Stra

Patricia H

Books by Patricia Rushford

Young Adult Fiction

JENNIE McGRADY MYSTERIES
1. *Too Many Secrets*
2. *Silent Witness*
3. *Pursued*
4. *Deceived*
5. *Without a Trace*
6. *Dying to Win*
7. *Betrayed*
8. *In Too Deep*
9. *Over the Edge*
10. *From the Ashes*
11. *Desperate Measures*
12. *Abandoned*
13. *Forgotten*
14. *Stranded*

Adult Fiction

Morningsong

HELEN BRADLEY MYSTERIES
1. *Now I Lay Me Down to Sleep*
2. *Red Sky in Mourning*
3. *A Haunting Refrain*
4. *When Shadows Fall*

Stranded

Patricia H. Rushford

Stranded
Copyright © 2001
Patricia H. Rushford

Cover illustration by Sergio Giovine
Cover design by Lookout Design Group, Inc.

Library of Congress Cataloging Card Number applied for

ISBN 0-7642-2122-1

Published by Bethany House Publishers
A Ministry of Bethany Fellowship International
11400 Hampshire Avenue South
Bloomington, Minnesota 55438
www.bethanyhouse.com

Printed in the United States of America by
Bethany Press International, Bloomington, Minnesota 55438

A special thanks to Ruby and Tom MacDonald,
who provided a beautiful sanctuary in which to write.
To Marcia Mitchell and my husband, Ron,
whose flying experience proved invaluable.
To my Round Robin friends
for their undying support and encouragement.

PATRICIA RUSHFORD is an award-winning writer, speaker, and teacher who has published numerous articles and more than thirty-five books, including *What Kids Need Most in a Mom,* and *Have You Hugged Your Teenager Today?* She is a registered nurse and has a master's degree in counseling from Western Evangelical Seminary. She and her husband, Ron, live in Washington State and have two grown children, seven grandchildren, and lots of nephews and nieces.

Pat has been reading mysteries for as long as she can remember and is delighted to be writing a series of her own. She is a member of Mystery Writers of America, Sisters in Crime, Romance Writers of America, and several other writing organizations. She is also the co-director of Writer's Weekend at the Beach and teaches at writers' conferences and schools across the country.

1

"You're doing a great job, Jennie. Flying like a pro." Jennie McGrady's grandmother, Helen Bradley, leaned over to peer out the window of her small plane, intent on taking aerial photographs of a large settlement they'd just passed over. "I'm almost done."

Jennie shielded her eyes from the overhead sun. "Looks like a storm up ahead."

"So much for the weather forecast." The camera clicked and whirred as Gram took several more shots. "Let's make one more circle."

Jennie made a right turn, lowering the right wing tip to give Gram a better view. The plane suddenly dipped as they hit a pocket of unstable air. Jennie yelped but managed to steady the plane.

"Are you okay?" Gram lowered the camera. "Do you need me to take over?"

"No. I'm fine." Jennie's confidence returned as she momentarily put the clouds behind her. She almost wished she hadn't talked her parents into letting her go with Gram. She could have driven with them, but she'd thought flying would be much more exciting. It was exciting, all right. Nail-biting time—that is, if she could get her hands off the controls to do it.

Once she made the circle and was back on course, her earlier concerns returned. "M-maybe we should turn back." Jennie gripped the controls harder as the clouds enveloped the red Piper Cherokee. Rain pelted the windshield. Thunder rumbled and exploded like a bomb, and a streak of lightning to the east ripped through the clouds. The plane rocked and pitched like a child's toy, mocking Jennie's efforts to keep it steady.

Gram tossed her camera aside and took over. "Hold on, sweetheart. I'll try to get us out of this mess." She made a left turn away from the storm and eased back on the throttle to lower their altitude. The turbulence subsided a little, but the rain continued to slash against the windshield.

"That's better," Gram said.

"It doesn't look better. We're still in the clouds, and I can't see anything."

"That's what the instruments and charts are for. We don't necessarily need to see."

"I know, but it's still scary." Jennie thought back to the day before, when Gram had invited her to fly to eastern Oregon with her. Mom hadn't wanted her to go, but Gram managed to convince her that it would be safe. And it should have been. When they left Lincoln City that afternoon, the weather reports had promised a perfect November day. Temperatures in the fifties, clear skies with a slight chance of rain. They should have known better than to believe it.

They were flying to Sun River, where they would meet J.B., Gram's new husband, and drive to Mount Bachelor to meet up with the rest of the family for a ski vacation—a gift from Gram and J.B. When Gram had said she was flying over, Jennie jumped at the chance to go with her. That morning, once the flight plan had been filed, Jennie had watched in anticipation as Gram checked over the plane and climbed into the cockpit. Her stomach had knotted with excitement and nerves at the thought of actually piloting the plane for short intervals while Gram coached her.

Jennie's stomach ached now as well—not in anticipation, but in dread. The cloud ceiling had lowered, engulfing them once again in the storm. Not wanting to think about the storm, she focused on what she thought was the real reason for the flight.

"I'm sorry." Jennie's words hung on an anxious sigh. "I hope you got your pictures."

"Sorry?" Gram gave her a puzzled look. "For what?"

"For needing you to take over flying." Feeling a chill under her jacket, Jennie rubbed her arms. "I should have been able to handle it."

Gram shook her head. "Sweetie, you've only had three lessons. Even experienced pilots can get caught off guard in this kind of weather."

"Yes, but—"

"No buts. You did fine."

Jennie didn't feel fine. She felt like she'd botched an assignment. "Did you get the pictures you needed?"

"Almost. It'll have to do," Gram answered.

"Why were you taking them, anyway?"

Gram gave her a sideways glance that said, "You know better than to ask."

"You're doing another job for the FBI?" When Gram didn't answer, Jennie dug deeper. "The DEA?"

Gram sighed. "Can't say. Strictly hush-hush."

Jennie grinned. "I'm right. It's the DEA. What is it? I won't say anything."

"That's right, because you don't know anything." After checking her charts and completing her instrument scan, Gram peered through the windshield, though Jennie didn't know why she bothered. Outside there was nothing but gray.

Not wanting to think about the weather, she pursued with the questions. "It's drugs, isn't it? Is there a meth lab down there?" Jennie raised her eyebrows. "I'll bet they're growing marijuana in that big greenhouse we saw."

"You're letting your imagination run away with you.

Don't you think it's entirely possible that I'm taking photos for an article?"

"Possible. But not likely. I mean . . . who'd want to vacation there?" Gram wrote for travel magazines and was always taking photos of exotic places. The place she'd been photographing was not what Jennie would have termed exotic or glamorous. More like weird. "It's a religious settlement, isn't it?"

"Yes. Settled in the late 1800s by a German colony of believers."

"So are they having trouble? Is the federal government closing in? Are they a cult? I saw something on television. Two guys from there were killed." Jennie leaned forward, trying to read Gram's face. "That's it, isn't it? You're taking pictures for the FBI. You're working on the murder investigation."

"Jennie . . ."

The warning in Gram's voice caused Jennie to momentarily give up her quest. Gram would tell her eventually. Maybe. Jennie leaned back in her seat, watched the rain turn to sleet, and pouted.

Jennie was used to the secrets. She didn't like them, but with their family it was a way of life. Her dad had worked with the Drug Enforcement Agency and was now a homicide detective. Gram had been a police officer and, since her retirement a few years ago, had taken up a career in writing. But she still took cases now and then and had been known to accept assignments from federal agencies. Her first husband, Jennie's grandfather, had been a government agent. He'd been killed on assignment in the Middle East. And J.B. was an agent too—or had been until a recent heart attack. Now he worked as a consultant.

"I need to check the weather and file an instrument flight plan." Gram tried contacting the control tower in Sisters to check the weather. The radio cut in and out. No voices. Only static. Muttering something unintelligible, she grimaced. "We're icing up."

The plane dipped, leaving Jennie's stomach behind. "Icing up? Does that mean we're going to crash?"

Gram didn't answer. "We've got to outrun this storm and try to get below freezing level. Hold on."

Jennie swallowed back the panic rising to her throat. She could see the solid coat of ice building up on the leading edge of the wings. Jennie didn't know much about flying yet, but she did know they were in trouble.

Gram banked to the right, taking them back the way they'd come.

"What does the ice do?" Jennie pinched her lips together and gripped her seat belt as though it were a lifeline.

"Basically, ice on the leading edge of the wings erodes the lift and makes the plane heavier. Gets sluggish . . . slower to respond . . . takes more power to hold the current altitude. Too much ice can cause the airplane to nose over, stall, and eventually crash." She glanced at Jennie. "I'm going to do all I can to make sure that doesn't happen."

As if in response to Gram's explanation, a loud siren wailed inside the cabin. "The stall warning!" Jennie yelled. The nose of the plane dropped, and the plane began spiraling. "What's happening?" Jennie braced her feet on the floor.

"We've gone into a spin." Gram pulled back on the yoke and leaned on her right foot, and with the increased speed, the plane began to level.

"You did it!" Jennie cheered.

"We're not out of the woods yet." Gram cast her a look of uncertainty. "Ice is still building."

The engine strained and groaned. The Cherokee dropped like a runaway elevator, leaving Jennie's stomach in midair. "Are we going to crash?" she asked again.

"Not if I can help it. We'll have to make an emergency landing."

"B-but how?" Jennie glanced out the window. "I can't

see anything but clouds and snow."

Gram checked her instruments, then pinched her lips together and grabbed Jennie's hand. Squeezing it hard, she said, "Pray," then turned her attention back to piloting the airplane.

Jennie did pray, but she wished she could do more. She knew how difficult landing would be. She'd seen enough news footage to know they might explode on impact. The eastern Oregon desert was filled with harsh, unforgiving rock formations. There were cattle ranches and the occasional field, but much of the land was as untamed as the wild horses that roamed there. If anyone could get them safely down, Gram could.

"We won't be able to see much until we're nearly on the ground. Hopefully we'll lose some of the ice buildup as we descend and get more lift from the wings."

By then it might be too late. Jennie squeezed her eyes tight and envisioned an open field. Maybe they were close enough to the compound they'd flown over. Hadn't there been an airstrip there?

"There was a landing strip back there. . . ." Jennie gave voice to her thoughts.

"I know." Gram shook her head. "We'd have to fly through a mountain to reach it."

Something exploded beneath them, rocking the plane with its force.

"What in the. . . ?" Gram's gaze registered terror. "We've been hit. Losing gas."

"What was it? Lightning? Did we hit a tree?"

Gram didn't answer.

A million thoughts went through Jennie's head as the plane plummeted. Would she ever see her mom and dad again? Or her little brother, Nick? She uttered a prayer of thanks that none of the rest of the family had come along. She worried about her mother. With losing the baby, Mom had been through too much already.

The envelope of clouds broke to reveal a rough, rocky

terrain. A grouping of scrub pines appeared in front of them. Instead of veering, Gram headed straight toward them.

"Gram!" Jennie screamed. "We're going to hit the trees!"

"We're going between them—I hope. I'll try to sheer off the wings to slow us down. Looks like there might be a level area just beyond them."

Jennie saw no reason whatsoever to slow down. They were already moving in slow motion—at least in her mind. Jennie prepared herself for the impact, leaning forward and covering her head. Gram aimed for the narrow space between the trees. A sickening crunch on either side of the plane attested to her success.

Success?

The plane lunged and whipped around before leveling out again. "This is going to be a rough one, honey. I'm so sorry. . . ." Before Gram could finish, the ground came up to meet them.

2

Huge boulders seemed to rise out of the ground to rip off the landing gear. The nose slammed into another outcropping of rocks, flipping the craft over, then over again. Jennie closed her eyes and waited for the terrifying ride to end. When the plane finally stopped, she raised her head and unfolded herself from the tight ball she'd curled herself into. Small, whimpering sounds filled her ears as her ragged breathing settled into a normal rhythm. Her sounds. Her cries.

Leaning her head back against the seat, she offered thanks to God for sparing her life.

Eventually Jennie's breathing became more shallow and slow. Her heart stopped racing. It was quiet now, except for the wind whistling through the cockpit. Too quiet. And dark. The heavily falling snow had already covered the windows, casting the cockpit into gray shadows.

"Gram?" Jennie ventured.

The only response came from the wind gusting against the plane.

In the dim light Jennie could see her grandmother's still form pressed against some rocks where the side of the plane had been torn away. "Oh no," Jennie whimpered. "Please, God, let her be alive."

The plane lay at an angle, with Jennie at the high side. Had it not been for the seat belt, she'd have fallen on top of her grandmother.

"Gram!" Jennie screamed it this time. "Wake up . . . please!"

Still no response.

Jennie covered her mouth to stifle the panic filling her throat, making it impossible to breathe.

Stay calm, McGrady. You have to stay calm. Jennie fought against her fears as she tried to remember her first-aid training. She took several deliberate breaths, deep and slow. "You can do this." She said the words out loud as she placed her fingers against Gram's throat.

"Please, God. Please." Jennie whispered the litany as she moved her fingers along Gram's jaw, searching for the carotid artery. Finally finding a pulse, Jennie allowed herself another deep breath again. "Okay." Jennie knew the routine. Now she just had to put it into practice. *Don't move her. Assess for injuries. Stop the bleeding. Keep her warm. First-aid kit.* After a moment's panic, Jennie remembered what Gram had told her about the first-aid equipment. *Behind the pilot's seat.*

Bracing herself, she released her seat belt and reached behind Gram's seat for a flashlight. Tears filled her eyes as she turned it on. Jennie blinked them back, trying not to be affected by the sight of her dear Gram lying there unconscious. *No time for crying. You have to stay in control. You can do this, McGrady. You have to.* Blood had dripped down Gram's forehead around her left eye and down her cheek, soaking into her white turtleneck. A closer look revealed that the blood was congealing and had stopped on its own. Jennie could see no other open wounds. Without moving Gram, Jennie had no way to check for further injuries. But at least she was alive—for now. Jennie wrapped Gram in one of the two emergency warming blankets and stepped outside. She needed air, and she needed to think.

Jennie paced back and forth beside the crumpled plane. Snow settled into the tops of her shoes and soaked her socks. Even with her ski jacket and hat, she felt cold and miserable. Conflicting messages whirled in her head.

Should she go for help or stay with the plane?

"What should I do?" She tipped back her head, looking for an answer. Snowflakes as big as quarters drifted down in silent response. "I don't know whether to stay here or go for help."

Try the radio. Jennie couldn't believe she'd been so stupid. That was one of the first things she should have done. Jennie climbed back into the cockpit and minutes later climbed back out. The radio was useless—no static, no nothing. She was on her own.

Pacing again, she weighed the options for the umpteenth time. Gram needed medical care now. She'd come to once but hadn't been coherent. The emergency transmitter in the tail section of the plane would send signals letting the authorities know they'd gone down, but would it do any good? As long as the storm continued, there would be no rescue attempts. On the other hand, Jennie knew they couldn't be far from the compound Gram had been photographing. Someone there would help.

Finally Jennie made up her mind. She couldn't stay with the plane when help could be over the next hill. Jennie estimated that she had about four hours of daylight left. She'd walk for two hours, and if she didn't find help, she'd return to the plane and wait. Jennie checked her location on the Global Positioning System. Pulling the instrument from the crumpled dash, she put it into her backpack. She'd be able to locate the plane easily. She changed into warmer clothes—a beige rag wool sweater over a turtleneck, gloves, and hiking boots. Jennie stuffed the emergency supplies she might need into her backpack.

She crawled back into the wreckage and kissed Gram good-bye. "I'll be back before it gets dark. Please be okay." Jennie set food and water within easy reach in case Gram awoke, then hauled in a deep breath. Assured that she was doing the right thing, Jennie walked away without looking back.

The wind had blown the snow in drifts, leaving some

places almost bare. About fifteen minutes into her hike, Jennie's jog had slowed to a brisk, breathless walk. Then she saw it—a trail marked by horse manure. Some was old and crumbly, frozen, but one pile looked fresh and had melted the snow around it. It still had a slight manure smell. She estimated that it couldn't have been there for more than an hour.

Jennie searched the ground looking for tracks but found nothing to indicate which direction this horse had gone. There were tracks going both directions.

"Which way, God?" Jennie stuffed her gloved hands into the pockets of the ski jacket. Jennie envisioned the religious compound again and kept going in the northeast direction she'd settled on at the plane.

By three o'clock, Jennie was ready to turn back. The sky had turned dark as dusk. Snow fell in slanting sheets, whipping against her face. Once again Jennie fought off the rising panic. What if she froze to death? It might be spring before her body was found. If it ever was.

She pinched her eyes shut. *"Get a grip, Jennie,"* she could almost hear her grandmother's calm, reassuring voice say. *"You can't let yourself think that way. You'll be all right. Just think it through."*

Jennie nodded in response to her invisible guide. She had to find shelter and fast. About fifty feet off the side of the trail, Jennie saw another large outcropping of jagged rocks. Snow lay in the crevices. Maybe she could find a nook to protect her from the wind. She left the trail and began climbing. The hill was steep and dangerously slippery. About twenty feet up, she stopped to rest on a ledge. "Maybe this wasn't such a good idea." The words had no sooner left her mouth than she spotted a dark, yawning opening a few feet to her right. A cave.

Jennie clambered across the rocks and crawled inside. It was larger than she'd expected. She brushed off the snow and removed her backpack. The wind moaned as it tore across the cave's narrow mouth. Reaching into her pack, she removed the flashlight she'd taken from the plane. She turned it on and shone it against the walls as she turned in a slow circle. The cave was good sized— about ten feet wide and fifteen feet deep. A stack of fire-wood leaned against one wall. Someone had built a fire in the center. Jennie couldn't tell how long ago it had been.

"All the comforts of home," she murmured. "Oh, Gram. I wish you were here with me. I shouldn't have left you." Facing the opening, she dropped to her knees. Hot tears trickled down her icy cheeks. "I should have stayed with the plane." She tried to imagine Gram safe and warm inside the cockpit. Snow would build up around it, making a snow cave. "She'll be okay," Jennie reassured herself again and again. As soon as the storm let up, she'd head back to the wreckage.

Several times during the next two hours, Jennie tried to set out, but each time the blinding snowstorm and com-mon sense drove her back. By nightfall, she had to accept the inevitable. She wasn't going anywhere until morning.

With the dry firewood someone had left and matches from her survival pack, Jennie built a fire. Exhausted, she took off her jacket and bunched it up for a pillow. Remov-ing a silver emergency blanket, she stretched out on the uneven, rocky floor and covered herself with it.

For a long time Jennie watched the fire and listened to the wind. "Please, God," she pleaded, "let Gram be okay. Help me get back to her. And please let someone find us."

She tried to imagine her family and how worried they would be. J.B. would be frantic by now. They'd been due in at the airport at four that afternoon. J.B. was to have picked them up and taken them to the cabin. Mom and Dad would already be there. J.B. would contact Dad on his cell phone. They would do whatever it took to find them. She took comfort in those thoughts and closed her eyes.

She'd almost fallen asleep when she heard a gunshot. Jennie bolted upright. Had she heard right? Her mind raced with possibilities. Who would be shooting out there at night? In a storm? Someone from the religious settlement? Another murder?

Jennie searched her mind for details of the story she'd seen on television about the two members from the religious group who'd been killed. They'd been shot, their bodies found in the desert. During the interview, a spokesperson for the group had called it a hate crime. He'd insisted that there were " . . . *enemies—outsiders intent on closing us down.*" Jennie stoked the fire, trying to remember more.

The spokesperson had been a handsome man with dark hair and kind eyes. In his forties, maybe, wearing a suit and tie. Nothing out of the ordinary about him. She'd been watching the news with her mom and dad. Mom had commented, *"Why can't they leave those poor people alone? It seems like everyone is a target of prejudice these days. It's not as if they're a cult. They're Christians. They worship the same God we do."*

"We don't know that for sure," Dad had said.

Dad's comment took on an ominous ring now. Had he known something about the deaths of the two men? As a homicide investigator he might, but this was way out of his jurisdiction.

Jennie wished she'd paid more attention, but the incident had come and gone as the newscasters went on to other stories. A religious order in the high desert hadn't interested her much at the time.

Another gunshot jolted Jennie out of her thoughts. This one seemed closer. Fear tied Jennie's stomach into hard knots. She thought briefly about stepping outside the cave to have a look around, then thought better of it.

A horse whinnied nearby, spurring Jennie into action. Staying low, she forced her feet to move toward the cave entrance.

"It's all right, Sable." The man sounded breathless and maybe frightened. "Settle down."

Were the shots meant for him? Was he from the settlement? Could he be meant as the next victim?

Maybe he wasn't a victim at all. Suppose he was the killer, and the sheriff was after him?

Jennie's heart hammered in her chest. She peered outside but saw nothing but swirling snow. She heard no sound except the wind. Had she imagined it?

No way. What if there's a criminal out there and he spots the cave? What if he's the one who put the firewood in here? Maybe it's a hideout.

Jennie tried to curb her overactive imagination, but it didn't work. She grabbed a stick from the log pile and backed against the cave wall beside the entrance. If he did come in, she'd be ready.

Ready for what? Jennie's common sense seemed to argue. *If he is a criminal and has a gun, the stick isn't going to do much good.* She tried not to think about how vulnerable and isolated she was. Instead, she imagined herself bringing her weapon down hard on the head of the intruder, then escaping out of the cave and running back to the plane. Maybe, if she was lucky, the guy would ride away.

The firewood popped. Jennie jumped. *Oh no.* Flames flickered higher. Hot coals rose like a fireworks display. Jennie's already-tight stomach knotted even harder. *I should have scattered the fire.* The light would shine out of the darkness like a beacon, welcoming the stranger. Too late now. Her breath held as she heard rocks falling. Boots scraped against the ledge. Jennie stifled a scream as a large, dark form ducked inside.

3

Jennie plastered herself against the cave wall and raised her club.

"What the . . ." He must have sensed her presence as he spun around just as she brought her weapon down. She'd aimed at his head and instead grazed his raised arm. With lightning speed he wrenched the stick away and lunged at her. The stranger froze when he saw her face.

They stared at each other for a long time before speaking. He seemed as surprised as she. Jennie took a step back. He was young—maybe a year or two older than she—and taller by several inches, making him over six feet. He wore a cowboy hat and an Australian moleskin coat that brushed the ground.

His questioning gaze searched her face. "Don't be afraid. I'm not going to hurt you." Dropping the stick, he added, "You surprised me, that's all."

"I . . . I . . ." Jennie stammered, trying to find her voice. She relaxed a little and moved toward the fire. "I'm sorry. I wasn't expecting company. Who are you, and what are you doing here?"

A wide grin spread across his handsome features. "I was going to ask you the same thing. I'm Eric. And you are. . . ?"

"Jennie."

"Well, Jennie, I was on a mail run. I stay here sometimes. Had hoped to make it back home before dark, but the storm . . ." He hesitated, eyeing her backpack. "You must have gotten caught in it too. Were you out hiking or something?"

"No, my—our plane crashed and—"

"Plane crash?" He frowned. "I was right. I heard it. Tried to find it, but the visibility is terrible. Finally gave up. I thought I'd hole up here tonight and look again tomorrow. Are you okay?"

"Yeah, um . . . just a few bruises. My grandmother is still out there." Jennie gazed into the fire. "I should have stayed with her. She's badly hurt."

"You were pretty brave to venture out here alone."

"Brave? More like stupid. We saw that religious compound from the air. I thought I was close enough to walk it. . . ."

"You are. That's where I'm from. It's only another five miles."

"You're a member of . . . of . . ."

"A religious order?" He smiled again, banishing Jennie's remaining fears. "You seem surprised."

"I am. The way you're dressed, I thought you were a rancher."

"I am—sort of. We dress pretty much like everybody else. At least I do. I take care of the horses." Eric hunkered down by the fire.

"Your horse." Jennie glanced toward the cave's mouth. "Will it be all right out there?"

"Sable?" He nodded, a look of pride on his face. "Sable's been through worse than this. She could have gotten us home, but I needed to stop."

"Won't they worry about you when you don't show up?"

He chuckled softly. "We don't worry about anything at the Desert Colony. Christ told us not to be anxious. We take that seriously. The Lord will provide all our needs. We must simply trust."

"Trust," Jennie murmured. "Sometimes it's hard. I

know I need to trust God to look after my grandmother, but I'm still worried."

"Will your worries and anxieties help her?"

Jennie smiled. Never in a million years did she imagine she'd be sitting in a cave in the high desert talking about religion with a guy she'd been terrified of only moments before. "No," she answered. "Of course not. It's just . . . I can't help it."

"It takes time and practice to learn such trust."

Jennie jumped up and began pacing. "I can't believe we're having this conversation. There's a storm outside. We don't even know each other. Gram is . . . I hate to think what might be happening out there."

Eric lifted his gaze to hers and held out his hand. "Put your fears to rest, Jennie."

"It's not that easy." Oddly, she felt some of her fears drain away as he spoke. She felt drawn to him. Taking his offered hand, she allowed him to guide her back to the fire.

"Sit beside me."

Jennie sat. Something in his tone calmed her. He exuded a kind of peace, a spiritual depth she hadn't experienced with any of the guys she'd known.

When she'd settled beside him, he spoke again. "You must realize that even now our Lord is working in our lives."

"I suppose. I was able to walk out. Gram is still alive." Jennie brushed away a newly formed tear. "At least, she was."

"Are you a believer, Jennie?"

"If you mean do I believe in God, yes. I'm a Christian."

"And your grandmother?"

"She is too. Why?"

"Then you believe that no matter what happens, even if it's a bad thing, the end result will be good." His blue gaze caught and held hers. Taking her hand again, he added, "The Lord is already working to save your grand-mother."

"What do you mean?" Jennie looked back at the fire.

"You went out in search of help."

"And got caught in a storm."

"You found refuge."

"But Gram . . ." She turned back to him.

"We'll search for her tomorrow." Eric squeezed her hand in a reassuring gesture.

Jennie nodded. "You're right. It's just that . . . I love her so much. I can't bear the thought of her being out there alone."

"She's not alone. If, as you say, she is a believer, then the Lord and His angels are watching over her, just as they are watching over us. They led you to this place and brought me to console and protect you." Eric stood, then retrieved another piece of wood for the fire.

"Why don't you get some sleep. I'll keep watch."

"Keep watch? Are you afraid of something?"

"No," he answered, a little too quickly.

So Eric didn't have the trust thing down completely either.

"I heard gunshots before you came in," Jennie remembered. "Was someone shooting at you?"

"No, I . . . I doubt it." Concern etched lines in his forehead. "I just don't want to take any chances."

"Why don't you just trust God?" A smile tugged at the corners of her mouth. "Sorry, I couldn't resist."

Eric sighed. "I do trust Him. But I don't trust humans. And, as you say, trusting isn't always as easy as we'd like it to be. Two of our members were shot to death last week. We think it may have been one or more of the ranchers." His jaw clenched. "I think I know who, but Donovan says we shouldn't judge—that we need proof. They don't like us. Donovan says it's because they don't understand our ways. He's doing all he can to protect us."

"Who's Donovan?"

"Our leader. You'll like him. He is the kindest and most spiritual man I have ever met."

Danger signals darted through Jennie's mind, but she wasn't certain why. "Are you sure those gunshots weren't aimed at you?"

"The shots were too far away." Eric started toward the mouth of the cave. "I'm going to check on Sable. You should get some sleep."

Jennie didn't feel like sleeping but opted not to argue. She snuggled back under her silver blanket, staring into the fire. Though she wondered about the Desert Colony and worried about Gram, she felt a strange sense of calm. Eric was right. She could trust God to take care of Gram—and her.

The next morning, Jennie climbed up on Sable's back behind Eric. "I still think we should go back to the plane. I have the GPS. We wouldn't have any trouble finding it."

"We'd be wasting time." Eric sounded less than spiritual this morning. They'd been arguing for ten minutes. Exasperated, he nudged Sable forward. "If we found her, we'd still have to go back to the compound to get something to transport her on. We have a doctor there. He'll go out with the men. They'll be much better equipped to take care of her than we are."

"She's been out there too long already."

"My point exactly. Trust me on this, okay?"

Eric's plan made sense. As Sable picked up her pace, Jennie wrapped her arms around Eric's waist and leaned her head against his back. Unbidden tears dripped onto his waterproof coat. *Please, God,* she prayed. *Please take care of Gram. Keep her safe . . . and alive.*

4

An hour later, Jennie and Eric arrived at the Desert Colony. High white walls surrounded it. Coiled barbed wire sat atop the wall. "It looks like a prison." Jennie felt relieved when Eric bypassed the worn path to the high iron gate.

"Looks are deceiving." Eric still sounded gruff, and Jennie didn't know if he was still mad at her for arguing with him or just tired from so little sleep. When she'd awakened, he was already up and putting out the fire. "Donovan had the wall built to protect us from the outsiders. Not to keep us in. We don't like it, but it's necessary."

"Why build a wall? I thought you believed that God would protect you." Jennie couldn't resist the jab—especially after all his preaching on not being anxious about Gram. While she did believe in God's protection, she also believed in doing everything humanly possible.

Eric didn't answer, and Jennie decided to drop it. "Where are we going?" she asked.

"Stables."

At the back of the compound stood a long building of white stucco and a red tiled roof. Beside it was an empty corral. An old-fashioned buckboard with a horse harnessed into it stood just outside the wide doors. The impressive stables reminded her of pictures she'd seen of large estates owned by horse breeders. "How many horses do you have?"

29

"Varies. Right now twenty." At the entrance to the stables, Eric helped Jennie down, then swung out of the saddle. He tied Sable to a hitching post and stroked the horse's neck. "I'll be right back, girl."

Taking Jennie's elbow, he propelled her around and steered her back to the front gate. There, Eric dropped her arm and told her to sit on a bench near the entrance and wait for him. "I need to get permission to bring you in," he explained.

"Why?" Jennie questioned, but Eric didn't answer. She started after him, but something held her back. She didn't like the barbed wire and had a strange feeling that once people entered they might not come out. It wasn't a rational thought. After all, Eric said the residents could come and go as they pleased. Still, Jennie's intuition told her things were not as wonderful at the Desert Colony as Eric made them out to be.

While she waited, Jennie tried to focus on her surroundings. The compound was a work of art. The inner grounds were beautifully kept. A three-foot band of green plants bordered the outside wall. The green stopped abruptly at the desert's edge. An oasis. Pristine patches of snow softened the contrast between the garden and the desert with its harsh, rocky soil and dry golden grasses. A tumbleweed bounced against the wall. Another gust of wind picked it up and tossed it toward Jennie. With a gloved hand, she batted it away.

At the sound of men's voices, Jennie jumped up and took several steps into the compound. Like a scene out of a wild west movie, Eric and three men strode toward the entrance and her. Each wore hats and moleskin coats. All but Eric carried saddlebags over their shoulders. Their coats hung open, revealing holsters and guns that hung on their hips.

"This is Jennie McGrady," Eric said as they drew near.

The largest of the men nodded and tipped his hat. "Stan."

"Daniel," said the next.

"Craig," offered the third.

Stan gave Jennie an empathetic smile, making him seem less intimidating. "Eric told us about your grandmother."

"It shouldn't be too hard to find her. I have the coordinates. We'll need medical supplies." Jennie gave them the GPS and told them where to find the plane. They didn't seem interested in hearing her coordinates. "How soon can we leave?" she asked.

The men looked at Eric, then back at Jennie. "We're riding out now," Stan said. "You stay here. Rest."

"No. I want to come. Gram needs me."

"We'll go alone."

"No way."

"You'll just slow them down, Jennie." Eric took hold of her arm.

Jennie pulled it away. "How? Why can't I just ride along?"

"They'd have to wait for you to saddle up."

"Saddle up? You're taking horses?"

"It's all we have." Eric gave her a patronizing look.

"I don't understand. She needs help right away. A four-wheel drive would be faster."

"We don't have a truck. There are no modern conveniences here, Jennie." Eric spread his hands in frustration. "It's our way."

"Well, your way stinks," Jennie sputtered. "I'm going anyway. I'll saddle my own horse. I don't care what you say, I'm coming with you." She leveled a challenging look at Stan.

"You'll stay here." Stan glowered at her. He apparently was not used to having his orders questioned. His bulk seemed to increase as he stared her down.

Glancing at Eric, he grumbled, "Take her to the women's dorm."

Eric took Jennie's arm again, and it was evident that

this time he had no intention of letting her get away.

"Wait, please." Jennie tried to pull away, but Eric held her firm.

"Stop fighting. It's for your own good."

Ignoring her protests, the men stalked away. At the gate, they turned left and headed for the stables.

"Why don't we just follow them?"

"Forget it. They're not taking you or me. Trust me, Jennie. They'll do better without us along. Come on. You must be hungry and tired. I am."

She was famished. All they'd eaten for breakfast was energy bars from her emergency rations. "Can I at least watch them leave?"

"You don't have to worry. They'll find her. They were already planning to go out."

"What do you mean?" Jennie started pulling Eric toward the gate.

"They knew about the plane before I told them."

"How?"

Eric shrugged. "Maybe they had a vision. Or they might have heard it go down like I did. If it hadn't been for the storm, they would have gone out yesterday. Anyway, the buckboard is already loaded with emergency supplies and the horses are ready."

"I thought you said there was a doctor. Is one of them a doctor?"

"No, but they've all had Red Cross training. They'll know what to do." Eric tightened his grip on her arm to restrain her.

As they reached the gates, the three men whipped by. Two, Daniel and Stan, were mounted on horses, while Craig drove an old buckboard wagon.

When she felt Eric's grip loosen, Jennie pulled away. For a moment she thought about getting a horse and going after the men despite orders, but she decided against it. They seemed capable enough. And Eric had a point. She probably would slow them down. God had answered her prayers and sent help. He'd brought her to a safe place. She had to trust that He would bring Gram back safely as well. She just wished their means of transportation were faster.

"Why are they taking horses? Don't you have trucks or something to use in an emergency? Going on horseback will take them forever."

"I told you. It's all we have. They don't have far to go."

"What about the airstrip? I saw it from the air. You must have planes. You could call Portland and have them send out a helicopter. They could life-flight her straight to the hospital."

"We don't have telephones. And we don't own any planes. The airstrip is provided for suppliers and export-ers."

"Exporters?"

"To take our products to the distributors."

"What products?" Jennie remembered again the aerial photographs Gram had taken. Were their "products" of in-terest to the DEA or the FBI? Fear knotted itself into a ball and settled in her stomach. The hair on the back of her neck stood at attention. What had she fallen into?

Eric smiled proudly. "We produce some of the world's purest herbs. Our products are shipped all over the world. That's where the money comes from to maintain this place."

"Herbs? Like what?"

He shrugged. "Like Echinacea, Saint-John's-wort— those are a couple of the most popular herbs. I'll show you around later."

Jennie straightened. It suddenly occurred to her that she was in a position to act as a secret agent. She'd infil-trated the ranks without meaning to. Had Gram been planning to become part of the sect to find out what they were really doing? Gram had always told her to make the most of any situation. She nodded, acknowledging Eric's response. "Sounds good."

"Come on. I'll take you to the women's dorm, where you can get a shower and some clean clothes. Then we'll have lunch."

They walked along one of many paths that curved and intersected like those you'd find on a college campus. All of the buildings were white with red roofs except for a large area covered by the huge dome she'd seen from the air. Jennie had a million questions about the place, but Eric told her they'd have to wait until they'd eaten.

A young girl stood at the entrance to the women's dorm. She was pale and thin, with enormous blue eyes and pale blond hair. She wore a simple soft blue dress with a high collar. She couldn't have been more than sixteen. Eric introduced her as Marilee.

"Welcome, Jennie." Marilee took her hand and brought her inside.

"I'll see you in the dining room." Eric waved and closed the door.

"Bye, Eric." Marilee bit her lower lip as she watched him leave. She had a high, melodic voice.

"Is he your boyfriend?" Jennie asked.

"Boyfriend?" Her cheeks flushed a bright pink.

"Are you going out with him?" Jennie tried again.

"You mean engaged?"

"Not exactly."

"Eric is not my intended. When I am of age, I will marry James." Marilee began walking down a long hallway. The white walls looked as though they had been freshly painted. Each door had a plaque with a Bible verse carved into it. Some of the doors had been left open to reveal one or two single beds with white sheets and dark gray blankets.

Jennie frowned. "But you like Eric. . . ."

Marilee pushed open the door to room 28. "We all like one another here."

"So is Eric *intended* for anyone?"

"He has not made his wishes known. Perhaps he will choose you."

Jennie frowned. "I'll do my own choosing, thank you. Besides, I'm not going to be here long enough to be chosen by anyone."

Marilee tipped her head as a look of confusion crossed her fair features. "You have not joined us, then?"

Jennie bit her lip. "My grandmother and I were on our way to Mount Bachelor for a ski trip. Our plane went down. Eric found me and brought me here so we could get help. I don't know much about this place. It seems interesting though. I'd like to learn more."

"Did Eric explain to you what we believe?"

Jennie nodded. "Mostly. You're Christians, right?"

"It is more complicated than that. We are of the old order. Different from most people who call themselves Christians."

"What makes you different?"

"While many on the outside claim to be believers, they do not live godly lives. They are not devoted followers of the Word."

"And the people here are?"

"We strive for purity." Marilee pointed toward the single bed and the clothes laid out on it. "When we join, we take a vow to give up everything that could have a corrupting influence."

"Like?"

"Television, radio, telephones. Any money or property we have is sold, and the money goes into our general fund. Most of us don't have a lot. I ran away from home when I was twelve. My parents drank and did drugs."

"How did you find this place?"

"James."

"Your fiancé?"

"Yes." Marilee's eyes brightened. "He was visiting the foster home where I had been placed. James told me about the Colony. He was so . . . perfect. I persuaded him to take me with him."

"You ran away with him? And you were only twelve?" Jennie's anger flared. "Recruiting kids that young has to be against the law. What did the authorities do?"

Marilee glared at her. "I chose to come. Donovan arranged things with the state. *He* is my father now. My parents were happy to be rid of me."

Jennie stared at Marilee in disbelief. "And you like it here?"

"Very much. For the first time in my life I have people who care about me. I have food and clothing and . . . soon"—she blushed—"I will have a husband."

"James. How old is he, anyway?"

"Ten years older than I." Her jaw clenched. "I know what you are thinking, Jennie McGrady, and you should be ashamed. James has always shown the utmost respect for me. When we met, he treated me as a sister. He was concerned and wanted me to have a better life. Over time we came to see that we were suited for each other. Donovan agrees."

Jennie pursed her lips. "You don't think he's too old?"

"Love has no boundaries."

"I . . ." Jennie started to argue but thought better of it. This wasn't the time or the place.

"The showers are across the hall. You'll find shampoo, soap, and towels there. I'll bring you a tray."

"Thanks."

By the time Jennie had showered and dressed and returned to the room, Marilee was waiting with a tray of food, which she'd placed on a small wooden table. Atop the table, a small vase of fresh flowers, a writing pad, and a Bible had been set to one side.

"The dress fits you well."

Jennie didn't think so. It was an old-fashioned ankle-length, high-necked dress, homemade from a simple floral print similar to what Marilee wore. "It's okay. I don't wear dresses much. Mostly jeans."

Marilee tossed a disapproving glance at Jennie's T-shirt and jeans. "They will be cleaned and returned when you leave. Until then, you will be expected to wear the clothing we provide."

"What about shoes?" Jennie pointed toward her hiking boots on the floor.

Marilee glanced at the boots and frowned. "Normally, you'd have to wear shoes like mine, but I couldn't find a size that would fit you, so those will have to do."

"Why can't I wear my own clothes?"

"It is not allowed." Marilee gestured toward the table. "I have brought your meal. It is simple stew and bread with one of our special health drinks."

"Health drink?"

"We make it fresh for every meal. It's a wonderful blend of fruits, vegetables, and herbs." Marilee smiled at Jennie's grimace. "Everyone loves it." She headed for the door. "Donovan says you are to eat and rest. Then Eric will take you to see him."

"This Donovan guy . . . does he have a last name?"

"We are all brothers and sisters in Christ. We have no need for last names—they only create separations."

Jennie settled her tall frame into the wooden chair and began to eat. She took a tentative sip of the fruit and vegetable drink. Marilee was right. It tasted great. She downed the contents of the tall glass and started in on the stew. The homemade soup and bread reminded her of home, and Jennie wondered what her parents were doing. They'd be frantic by now. Would they be able to find the plane? Glancing out the window, she saw that it was still snowing. She ate quickly and pushed the tray aside.

Lethargy settled over her like a heavy blanket. To dispel it, Jennie got up, then stretched and twisted from side to side. She didn't have time to sleep. Had to find out if they'd found Gram. Had to talk to the head guy and find out more about the herbs.

She staggered toward the door and twisted the doorknob. It wouldn't open.

5

They'd locked her in.

"Marilee!" Jennie banged on the door and shouted, "Let me out of here!"

No one came. Jennie fumed in indignation. How dare they lock her in. She tried the door again.

"Eric!" She tried yelling at him, too, but doubted he'd come to her rescue in the women's dorm.

"You can come and go as you please," he'd said. Had he lied to her? Was she a prisoner? She tried the window but found it opened only six inches, which did her no good at all.

A few minutes later her anger subsided. *Rest.* That's what Marilee had said she should do before meeting Donovan. Was this their way of making certain she followed orders?

Despite her irritation, Jennie yawned and crawled onto the narrow bed. Within minutes she was asleep.

———

Jennie woke up cold and shivering. She reached for her own fluffy comforter, but it wasn't there. Instead, her hand closed around a rough wool blanket. Sitting up, she yawned and rubbed her eyes. It took several moments to orient herself. She'd fallen asleep on top of the blankets and left the window open. Someone, probably Marilee, had locked her in. Jennie rolled off the bed, tangling her legs in the folds of the long skirt. Irritated, she untangled herself and went to close the window. The sky was an eerie yellow gray. Glancing at her watch, she winced. It was already after four and getting dark.

The men should be back. Had they found Gram?

Jennie ran a hand through her long hair as she hurried to the door. She had to pull hard, but this time it opened. Had it been locked before? Or had it just been stuck? Jennie's memory was fuzzy. Maybe she hadn't tried hard enough to open it.

She crossed the hall to the bathroom. Splashing cool water on her face helped clear her head.

Marilee stepped into the bathroom. When she spotted Jennie, she smiled. "Hi. Looks like you really needed that nap."

"Humph. Maybe so, but I don't appreciate being locked in."

A look of surprise crossed her features. "Oh, but I didn't—" She stopped short.

"Maybe you didn't, but someone did."

"You must be mistaken." Marilee smiled. "Some of the doors in the older buildings have a tendency to stick."

"Right. Forget it." Jennie grabbed one of the neatly folded hand towels on a shelf and dried her face. The door had been hard to open, but still . . . Jennie tossed the incident aside. It didn't make sense that anyone would want to lock her in. No sense at all.

"Um . . . we're having afternoon prayer. Would you like to join us?"

"I thought I was going to meet Donovan." Jennie ran a brush through her hair and secured it in a loose knot on top of her head.

"Yes, but you slept past your meeting time. He has invited you and Eric to dine with him. Eric will take you to his quarters after prayer."

Jennie and Marilee walked side by side down the long hall. "Sounds like they've already started," Jennie said.

"We begin at four. Donovan thinks it's important that we stay on schedule." Marilee directed Jennie through a set of double doors down another hall. "This is our common area. We gather here for meals and services and meetings. The men's dorm is on the other side."

"Have they come back—the men who went to look for my grandmother?"

"Um . . . yes."

Jennie's stomach lurched at the hesitation in Marilee's voice. Something had gone wrong. "Did they find her?"

"I really can't say." She paused at the open double doors. The singing increased in volume.

"Why?"

"Donovan will speak with you." She placed a hand on Jennie's shoulder. "Whatever happens, Jennie, I'll be here for you. Just remember, all things work for good in accordance with God's will."

Jennie wanted to shake her. What couldn't she tell her? Jennie wanted to yell—insist she be taken to Donovan immediately—but she didn't. She had to keep her cool. Had to observe these people. Had to stay alert—for Gram.

The room they entered looked like a church sanctuary. A beautiful stained-glass window adorned the front wall. The last of the sun's rays filled the room with a myriad of colors. A large cross draped with a white cloth hung from the ceiling. There was an altar in the center and a pulpit to the left of it. A kneeling rail framed them.

About a hundred people knelt on kneeling benches in the pews. The women were all dressed in the same style clothing that Jennie and Marilee wore. The men wore trousers and white shirts. Their dress and mannerisms reminded Jennie of photos she'd seen of the Amish.

Eric spotted them and moved farther into the pew, beckoning them to join him.

"Did you rest well?" he whispered as she stepped in beside him. He handed her an open hymnal.

"Someone locked me in," she hissed, "and I didn't appreciate it."

He frowned. "You must be mistaken."

"Humph." Jennie didn't know whether to believe him or not.

He turned his attention to the hymnal and began to sing along with the group. Training and familiarity with the songs moved Jennie to sing. She entered into the worship like she might have at home. She had a lot to talk to God about.

When the service ended at five, Jennie asked Eric about her grandmother. "Marilee acted like they hadn't found her. Did they? Do you know?"

"Take it easy, Jennie. You need to trust God in this."

"I do. I just want to know what happened."

"You will. I'll take you to Donovan right now."

"Good." Jennie's heart hammered in anticipation. Finally she'd be meeting the man in charge. She'd get some answers. So why did the idea of meeting him frighten her?

Eric escorted Jennie out of the great room and across the grounds into another building—a smaller one resembling a private home. As with the others, this building was also white stucco with a red roof. Just above the door hung a small wooden cross.

They stepped into a tiled entry. Beyond it, Jennie could see the hardwood floors and beige area rugs. When she started toward the living room, Eric held her back. With his free hand he pulled a cord, and a gong sounded.

"You can't just walk in," he explained. "Donovan may be in a private session."

"Welcome, dears." An elderly woman with stooped shoulders stepped into view. Her gray gaze moved from Eric to Jennie. "You must be Jennie."

"Yes . . . I—"

"Come in. Come in." Her warm smile put Jennie at ease. "Donovan is expecting you."

"This is Lois." Eric gave the woman a hug. "She's been here for over sixty years."

"Seventy." Her eyes sparkled. "I was born here. My father was one of the founders."

Jennie felt enormous next to the tiny woman. "Wow. You must like it here."

"Yes."

Was it Jennie's imagination, or had some of the sparkle gone out of the woman's eyes? "I'd like to hear about how you came to be here and how all this got started."

Lois seemed pleased. "Then you must come and have tea with me. Perhaps tomorrow. Eric can show you to my room."

"Do you stay here?"

"Oh no, dear. I'm in the women's dorm." She turned and started walking into the living room. Seated on the couch in front of the fireplace were two of the three men Jennie had seen that morning—Stan and Daniel. Reading their expressions of pity sent Jennie's heart skittering into a black hole.

Somewhere in the distance she heard her name.

A man wearing a loose-fitting white shirt and khaki pants took her hands. "Welcome to our humble community."

Jennie tore her gaze from the men on the sofa to focus on Donovan. She recognized him as the spokesperson she'd seen on the television interview. He was shorter than she'd expected. Stocky, tan, with coffee brown hair and eyes that seemed to change color even as he watched her. Gray, green, blue.

"I'm sorry it has to be under such tragic circumstances," Donovan went on.

"Tragic . . ." Her voice trailed off. She bit her lip and took a deep breath. "Did you find my grandmother? Is she—?"

"Perhaps it would be best if we spoke privately." He nodded a dismissal at the men and Eric.

"Wait!" Jennie grabbed hold of Eric's shirt. "I want Eric to stay."

"Very well." To the men he said, "We'll continue our discussion in the morning."

When they left, Donovan gestured for Jennie to sit down. Lois came into the room with a pitcher of juice and glasses. She poured a glass for each of them. Donovan and Eric picked theirs up. Donovan handed the remaining glass to Jennie. She shook her head. "Please. I want to know about my grandmother. Why can't you just tell me?"

"As you wish." He took a long drink and set his glass on the table. "Stan, Daniel, and Craig found the wreckage."

"And Gram. . . ?" Jennie braced herself, not wanting to hear the news they seemed so reluctant to give, yet needing to.

"She wasn't there."

6

"What?" Jennie didn't know what she'd expected, but it wasn't this. "What do you mean she wasn't there?"

"The men searched the area but could find no one. It is possible she was rescued, though there weren't any signs of that. She most likely walked out." Donovan reached down beside the couch and pulled up Gram's suitcase and her black leather backpack. "My men found these. Thought you might like to have them."

A lump in her throat stopped her response. Jennie took the backpack and ran her hand along the soft leather. *Gram is alive. She has to be.* "She wouldn't have left this behind. If she'd been rescued, she'd have taken her pack. And she'd never have left on foot without provisions and survival gear."

"Eric mentioned that she'd had a head injury. Perhaps she came to and wandered off."

"No." Jennie gripped the bag. "She wouldn't do that. She's trained—"

"Trained?" Donovan cast her an odd look.

"Um . . . to take care of herself." Jennie pinched her lips together. "She's had wilderness survival training."

"I see." Donovan lifted his glass and took a drink. "I'm afraid we can only guess what has happened to her. But we can pray that she remain alive and safe."

"Someone should be looking for her." Jennie tightened her grip on the pack's strap.

"Ah, but they are. While my men were out, they alerted the authorities. The sheriff has promised to continue the search and to locate your family. You must not be anxious, Jennie. Trust in the Lord to bring about His perfect will."

"Why didn't the sheriff come get me?"

"What would be the point? You're safe here. As soon as they locate your parents, you'll be returned."

Jennie swallowed back her frustration. It would do no good to argue. And against what? They'd done everything they could. Well, maybe not everything. They hadn't let her search for Gram. "I'd like to go back to the wreckage."

"I'm not sure that's wise."

"It's not that I don't trust you. I just need to see for myself. Maybe I can find something your men missed. Some clue as to where she might have gone."

He sighed heavily. "There's really no point."

"Maybe not, but I have to."

"I could take her." Eric glanced warily at Donovan. "I should make a mail run again tomorrow anyway."

Donovan relented. "You are free to do as you wish, of course, but I strongly advise against it. The weather conditions are still poor. There's another storm predicted tonight."

Jennie sucked in a deep breath and let it out in a rush. "Good. How early can we start, Eric?"

"Um . . . like Donovan said, we need to see what the weather's like tomorrow. If it's snowing . . ."

"I know." Jennie sighed. "I just wish you had a way for me to contact my family. Are you sure you don't have a phone or a computer. . . ?"

Donovan gave her a sympathetic look. "We prefer not to have modern conveniences here. I'm sure Eric explained that. We feel they compromise our standards."

"But you have an airstrip."

"Yes, unfortunately. If we are to survive here, we must receive food and supplies as well as get our products to

46

market. Planes are the most expedient way, as the road into the compound is not adequate for anything other than horses."

"And four-wheel drives," Jennie murmured.

"None of which would be large enough to serve our purposes. As for the planes, we don't have any of our own," Donovan added, confirming Eric's earlier response. "We simply run and maintain the landing strip."

"But you have a hangar."

"Sometimes the pilots need to work on their planes or keep them out of the weather."

"What about a radio? Don't you have radio contact with the planes?"

"No." His Adam's apple rose and fell, showing his obvious frustration with her persistence.

"I already told her that." Eric looked like he was ready to throttle her.

She ignored him. "What happens when you have an emergency? If someone is hurt or . . . killed?"

"Sometimes I wish we did have a more effective means of communication. But if we relent in one area, what stops us from relenting in another? We must draw the line. The Bible tells us not to be conformed to the world and its ways."

Donovan had drawn a number of lines, and Jennie kept crossing them with more and more questions. She probably shouldn't push it, but their head-in-the-ground attitude made Jennie want to scream. "How can a phone be bad?"

Donovan straightened, seeming to set aside the matter. "I understand you are upset about your grandmother. It is a tragic thing. But let us not worry about tomorrow or the weather or what fate awaits us or Mrs. Bradley."

Jennie frowned. "How . . . how did you know her name? I didn't tell you."

Donovan nodded at the backpack. "Her ID is in her wallet."

"Oh."

Giving Jennie a warm smile, Donovan placed a hand at her back and escorted her into the dining room. "We can perhaps talk more about your grandmother later, but now it is past time to eat, and dinner will be getting cold."

Gram is more important than your stupid old dinner. Jennie bit her lip to keep her comment inside.

Entering the large dining room, Jennie set her anger aside. She was hungry, and the food smelled delicious. She was surprised to find a long, rectangular table surrounded by twelve chairs in the center of the room. The chairs were simple straight-backed Shaker style, yet the natural wood gave it a look of elegance. Fresh flowers filled two vases that sat on a starched white table runner. Three places had been set at one end. A large soup tureen, a bowl of salad greens, a basket of bread, and a pitcher filled with some kind of iced beverage waited for them. The smells made Jennie's stomach growl in anticipation.

Donovan held out the chair at the head of the table for Jennie. Then he and Eric sat on either side of her.

"Um . . . shouldn't you be sitting here?"

He smiled. "You are my guest. I trust you will do the honors and bless our meal."

Feeling a bit intimidated, Jennie asked the blessing. Normally prayer came easily for her. At home they said grace at nearly every meal. But this was different—like praying in front of a pastor.

Donovan thanked her and reached for a basket of freshly baked bread. After tearing off a portion, he handed it to Jennie. She slathered butter onto her piece and spent the next few minutes indulging herself in what had to be the best stew she'd ever eaten. The small bits of meat had the texture of hamburger, but not the taste. "This is good," she managed between bites. "What kind of meat is in it?"

"I'm glad you approve." Donovan smiled. "There is no meat in it. It's tempeh." At Jennie's questioning look he added, "A soy product that's specially treated."

"We make it here," Eric said, "for our own use. It's Donovan's secret recipe."

"Not mine, exactly, my mother's. We were primarily vegetarians long before it was popular. The tempeh satisfies most of the meat eaters among us."

By the end of the meal, Jennie felt satisfied and strangely at ease. Donovan was right. She needed to let her concerns go and place them in God's capable hands. God could take care of Gram far better than she could. Donovan, in his gentle and persuasive way, had helped her to see that. She'd still go riding with Eric in the morning, but she didn't feel the urgency about searching that she'd had before. *Peace,* Donovan had called it. *A peace that passes understanding.*

After thanking Donovan for the meal, Jennie and Eric left his quarters to go back to the dorms. Eric took hold of her hand as they walked.

Jennie wondered briefly about what Ryan and Scott would think of her being with Eric. Just as quickly she shrugged the thoughts away. They had both been boyfriends, but Ryan was currently dating Camilla and wanted to remain friends, and Scott was too busy working with whales to think much about her. She still liked them both, but she was beginning to like Eric as well.

"Well, what did you think?" he asked.

"About what?"

"Donovan, of course." Eric cast her a bemused smile. "Isn't he great? He has this way about him—you know, that calms people down. Gets them to let go of their problems."

"Hmm." Jennie had to agree. She felt more relaxed than she had in ages.

"Hey." Eric tightened his grip and pulled her toward the gates. "I have to check on the horses. Why don't you come with me?"

"Sure."

They walked through the open gates, and Jennie sensed an even greater freedom. She could come and go as she pleased. She frowned, remembering the locked door. *You must have been mistaken,* she told herself. *The door was just hard to open, that's all.* She drew in a deep breath. The air was cold and snowflakes drifted down. Jennie tipped her head back and caught some flakes with her tongue. A cool wind swirled around her ankles, lifting and tugging at the hem of her dress. She'd rather have been wearing her jeans, but the dress was okay. It made her feel feminine and old-fashioned, something she didn't mind at all.

"It's good you came to us, Jennie." Eric opened the barn door and stepped inside. Several horses snickered a greeting.

"Why's that?" The earthy smell of dirt and manure settled Jennie even more. She didn't know why she'd let her imagination run away with her like that. These were good people. Kind people. They'd welcomed her in and treated her like one of their own.

Eric went straight to the horse he'd been riding earlier and stroked her neck. She snorted and nuzzled him. "I don't think it was an accident. I think God knew you needed a respite, so He sent you to us."

"Actually, I do. But so does our whole family. Why didn't God send any of the others?"

"Who knows? Maybe you are more in need of what we have to offer here."

"I need something. Life hasn't exactly been easy lately. Especially for my mom and dad."

"What do you mean?"

"That's why we were going to Mount Bachelor. Gram and J.B.—my grandfather—arranged this ski vacation for us. Thought it might help us get over . . ." Jennie felt an overwhelming sadness. She hadn't thought about little Emily all day.

Eric stepped away from the horse and settled an arm around her shoulders.

Tears escaped Jennie's eyelids and trickled down her cheeks. "My little sister died in childbirth. She came too early."

"I'm sorry." Eric gathered her into his arms. Jennie wrapped her arms around his waist. These were the first real tears she'd shed for the baby. Between sobs she told Eric how her mom had gone into labor early, and Emily was just too little and too sick to survive. She leaned her head against Eric's chest, taking comfort in the steady beat of his heart. Her own heart ached with the loss of her sister and even more at the thought of what might have happened to Gram. *No*, she told herself. *Don't go there. Gram is strong. She can take care of herself.*

Jennie sighed. "I'm sorry. It's just . . ."

"Hey, no problem. Lois says tears help clean the heart."

She took a deep breath and stepped away. "I like that. Sounds like something Gram would say."

"Look." Eric pointed out the barn doors at a bright, nearly full moon. "It's clearing up. How about going for ride?"

"Can we do that?" Jennie smiled. Except for her trip to the Colony that morning, she hadn't been riding since last summer when she'd stayed at her aunt and uncle's dude ranch in Montana.

"Sure. It'll be fun. With the moon on the snow it'll be just like daylight."

She glanced at her skirt with disdain. "I don't know if I can ride in this dress."

"Sure you can. Just ride sidesaddle."

Jennie helped Eric saddle up Sable and another horse called Faith. Faith was a gentle mare with soft brown eyes and a disposition to match. At Jennie's request, they rode around the compound. Lights attached to the tops of the walls lit the periphery. She and Eric rode outside their reach.

"It still looks like a prison," Jennie mumbled.

"I guess in a way it does." Eric glanced warily at the shadowed hills surrounding them. "Like I told you, it isn't to keep us in. . . ."

"I know. It's to protect you. I'm still not sure from what." She followed his gaze over the hills. Coming around toward the stables, Jennie saw a flash of light about halfway up one of the higher hills. "What was that?"

Eric reined his horse in. "I don't know. Almost looked like lightning."

"But no thunder." Jennie pulled up beside Eric, then nudged Faith forward in the direction of the light.

"Jennie, don't. It might be—"

The unmistakable sound of a gunshot split the cold, clear night.

7

"Get down." Eric jumped off his horse and gave her a swat. Sable reared and broke into a run, heading back for the barn.

Faith whinnied and pranced anxiously to join Sable.

Following Eric's lead, Jennie managed to clear the saddle, then took cover behind an outcropping of rocks. Her heart hammered so loudly she could barely hear Eric's instructions to stay low and follow him. They moved among the rocks, managing to stay under cover for about twenty yards. Scrambling behind the last rocks at the bottom of the hill, Eric put up his hand to stop her. "Wait."

"Don't worry. I'm not going anywhere," Jennie panted. "Do you think they were shooting at us?"

"You don't see anyone else out here, do you?" Eric ran a hand through his dark hair. "I just wish they'd leave us alone."

"They?"

"The farmers around here. Bunch of rednecks who're scared out of their gourds that we might be some kind of quirky cult."

"And you're not?" Jennie winced. She hadn't meant to make the comment out loud. Unfortunately she often had a habit of speaking before thinking.

He grunted some comment she couldn't hear.

"I'm sorry."

"Hmm. We can talk about it later. Right now we've got

to get back inside the compound."

The distance to the barn had to be the length of a football field. With the moon spotlighting them, they'd give whoever was out there a clear shot.

"What do we do now?" Jennie scanned the distance.

"Wait and pray."

Jennie shivered as much from fear as from the cold. "I don't know. I think we should run for it." She crouched lower and peered around the rocks. "What's to keep them from coming after us?"

"I don't think they'll risk it. We're too close to the compound." Eric tapped her shoulder and pointed up. "Look. Clouds are starting to cover the moon. In a minute it'll be too dark for them to see us. We'll head for the barn."

"What about the lights? They'll see us for sure." Jennie had no sooner gotten the question out than the lights surrounding the compound went out. At the same time, the moon slid behind the clouds, casting the entire area into an inky black darkness.

"Let's go."

"Wait. It's too dark." Jennie no longer wanted to move, but Eric grabbed her hand again and pulled her forward. "Who turned out the lights?"

"Who cares? Probably someone inside heard the shot. It doesn't matter. Just think of it as an answer to prayer."

"Well, pray for a little light, then. I can't see a thing."

"Just hold on to me, and I'll get you to the barn."

Jennie stuck close to Eric, stumbling several times over the rocky terrain. Once inside, they took cover in an empty stall near the open barn doors. "Wait here," Eric ordered. "I'll make sure the coast is clear and find . . ."

His whisper faded. Jennie didn't much like being left alone and liked it even less when she heard a scuffling sound. At first she thought it might be a critter of some sort sharing the stall with her. A thud shook the timbers. A muffled groan and running footsteps told her the intruder was a lot more dangerous than any rat or coon.

What's going on? Eric, where are you? Talk to me. Jennie couldn't have spoken if she'd wanted to. She wasn't certain whether to stay put or go out to try to find Eric. "Eric?" she whispered.

A door creaked. Jennie ducked back into the stall. Peering around the corner, she saw a figure holding a flashlight emerge from an opening across the way. The flashlight beam jerked over the rough-hewn timbers.

"Eric?" a woman whispered. "Eric? Is that you?"

Jennie stepped out of the stall as soon as she realized who it was. "Lois?"

The older woman swung around, flashing the light on Jennie's face.

"Oh my." Lois stepped back. "Jennie. You frightened me half to death. Where's Eric? I thought I saw you two come out here earlier, and when I heard the shot I was afraid that . . ."

"Whoever shot at us missed. Eric is here . . . somewhere." Jennie glanced around. "Someone else was here too. I heard—" Jennie gasped as the flashlight beam landed on a still form sprawled out on the barn floor.

"Eric!" Both women rushed forward at once.

8

Lois shone the light on him while Jennie checked for a pulse. She found it just as Eric pushed her hand away. Groaning, he covered his eyes. "What happened?"

"I was hoping you could tell me." Jennie explained what she had heard.

Eric rubbed the back of his neck and sat up. "I remember now. I was going toward the door and heard footsteps. Some guy ran into me."

"You don't know who it was?"

"No. He swore at me and slammed me against the post. Must have knocked me out."

"Well, thank the Lord you're all right." Lois swept a lock of hair from his forehead. "We'd better get you to the infirmary. Let one of the nurses take a look at you."

"I'm fine." He frowned. "What are you doing out here?" he asked Lois.

"I heard the shot," Lois said. "I saw you and Jennie heading for the stables earlier. I was worried."

"You shouldn't have come. You should have asked one of the men."

"They were busy dousing the lights and locking the gate—and calming people down. Besides, I'm probably more familiar with the tunnels than they are."

"Tunnels?" Jennie looked from one to the other. "What tunnels?"

"We have an emergency escape route," Eric answered.

57

Jennie straightened and gave Eric a hand up. "This place gets stranger by the minute."

"We've had to develop security measures." Eric brushed off his jeans.

"It didn't used to be like this." Lois moved toward the trapdoor from which she'd come. "There were no walls or barbed wire. No locked gates and certainly no need for security. We lived peacefully with our neighbors."

"Times change." Eric sighed and began the descent into the abyss. Jennie followed at Lois's request, then turned to take the flashlight from Lois as the older woman pulled the door closed.

"I suppose you're right. The world is less tolerant now." Lois took the flashlight and led them through the small brick-lined cellar into another tunnel on the other side. The air smelled dank and earthy. Some kind of animal—a rat, probably—gave a protesting squeal and scurried away.

Jennie stuffed her hands in her pockets and hunched her shoulders. The passageway was about three feet wide and lined with concrete. Clean. No cobwebs that she could see. Jennie tried to paint a mental picture of where they might be in relation to the buildings. She imagined them going beyond the barn and across the yard from the stable to the compound.

After several minutes of walking, they came to a T. Lois hesitated a moment before turning to the left.

Jennie stood at the intersection, peering down the dark passageway. "Where does that one lead?"

"To Donovan's quarters and the warehouse." Lois kept walking. "It's linked to the hangar."

Jennie watched the light from the flashlight fade and hurried to catch up. Curiosity sent shivers up and down her spine. She made a mental note to ask Eric if they could come back later and explore the tunnels more thoroughly.

"There is an escape hatch from each building," Eric

explained as they walked along. "We even have a bomb shelter."

"A bomb shelter? Like big enough to hold everybody?" Jennie was beginning to feel claustrophobic and would have welcomed such a room.

"The shelter was built in the fifties, when people were worried about the threat of nuclear bombs," Lois explained.

"Sounds like you don't like it." Jennie brushed her hand against the cold, damp wall and cringed. Putting her hands back into her deep jacket pockets, she moved closer to Eric.

"I was against it at the time. We use it now to store our herbs before they are shipped out, so I suppose it wasn't a complete waste."

"Where is it? Can I see it?"

"Now?" Lois looked aghast. Turning, she lifted the light and met Jennie's gaze. "You're not serious."

"Um . . . not tonight, I guess. But I would like to see it."

"Maybe I could take you tomorrow." Eric grinned at her. "I'd have to ask Donovan, but I'm sure he wouldn't mind."

They came up in the kitchen off the common area between the men's and women's dorms. Lois turned out the flashlight and hung it on a peg in the pantry. "I don't know about you two, but I could use some herbal tea to settle my nerves."

"Sure," Eric agreed and took three cups from the huge cupboard. "Sounds good."

Jennie agreed. "My Gram and I have tea a lot. Actually, my whole family does. Gram says it soothes the nerves and helps you think more clearly."

"This is our special blend, Jennie." Lois filled a teakettle and set it on the stove, then pulled out a canister full of loose tea. "I'd like to meet your grandmother sometime. Sounds like a woman after my own heart."

"She's great." *And she's hurt and out there alone.* A lump lodged in Jennie's throat as unbidden tears formed.

"Don't you worry, dear." Lois patted her arm. "God will take good care of your grandmother."

Jennie paced the floor until the teapot whistled, then took the tea Lois offered and walked with them into the vast dining room.

"Where is everybody?" Jennie set her cup down at the end of one of the polished wooden tables.

"Probably asleep. Or at least in their rooms. Curfew is at ten, and it's nearly eleven now."

"How could anyone sleep? I mean, we've been shot at. Doesn't anybody care?"

"I doubt anyone knew you were out. Unfortunately, we hear shots like that about once or twice a week. It's frightening."

"Not to me," Eric said. "Just makes me mad. They're trying to scare us out."

Eric had been plenty scared, but Jennie didn't bother to remind him. Instead, she wrapped her hands around the hot pottery mug and drew in a deep breath. The tea smelled like fruit. It tasted fruity too, like raspberry with some chamomile.

"If it were only that simple." Lois paused to take a drink. "Two of our people have been killed. That's why I was so concerned about you and Eric. I imagine the authorities are trying to find the killers."

"Humph. They don't care about us. If those guys had poached a couple of deer, the sheriff would have them in jail already. We're no more important to them than a bunch of possums."

"Now, Eric, you're not being fair. The sheriff has been here several times asking questions."

"Yeah? Well, why isn't he arresting someone?"

"They have a suspect. Jake Adams."

Jennie felt Eric stiffen beside her. "I shouldn't be surprised," he said.

"Who's that?" Jennie ran a hand through her tangled hair.

"Our nearest neighbor," Lois explained. "The Adamses are nice people. Mrs. Adams comes by often to chat and see how we're doing." She gave Eric a critical look. "Seems to me you're being rather judgmental."

"Jake is the judgmental one." Eric gritted his teeth. "He hates this place."

"I don't believe there's been an arrest yet. To my knowledge there's no proof he or his father are involved." Lois glanced at Jennie as if to say they had no proof of anything. "Anger will get you nowhere."

A sullen Eric pursed his lips and fixed his gaze on the floor, his anger deflated. "You're right. I'm sorry."

As they drank their tea, Jennie felt herself relax again. She yawned several times, and Lois insisted they all go to bed. They brought their cups to the kitchen. Jennie was rinsing hers and setting it in the sink when Lois turned out the light. Her image in the window above the sink faded, allowing Jennie to see outside. It was dark except for a glow of lights above the wall. The hangar?

"Jennie?" Lois turned the light back on. "Are you all right?"

"Um . . . yes. I'm just curious about the lights. They seem to be coming from the hangar."

"There's probably a flight due in."

A plane coming in tonight. Jennie tucked the information aside for later. "When Eric and I went out riding, there were lights all around the compound. Who turned them off?"

"Most likely one of the men responsible for security. During the Second World War they used to have black-outs—all lights out so the enemy couldn't see where to aim their bombs. We've adopted a similar practice since the killings."

"It's supposed to keep us safe." Eric rubbed the back of his neck. "But I sure wish the lights had been on in the barn so I could have seen who hit me."

Jennie wished she could have seen him too. Had the man in the barn also been the shooter? After promising Lois he'd check in with a nurse before going to bed, Eric headed toward the men's dorm. Lois accompanied Jennie to her room and waited until Jennie had gone in and closed the door before leaving.

Jennie tried the door. It stuck a little but opened just as it had before. At least they hadn't locked her in. She shuffled over to the bed, where someone had laid out a cotton nightgown. After putting it on, Jennie went into the women's rest room to brush her teeth and use the toilet. Once back in her room, she reluctantly climbed into bed.

Although the tea had a calming effect on her nerves, her mind still churned. Twice now she'd heard gunshots. Once at the cave just before Eric showed up, and tonight while she and Eric were riding. It made no sense that someone would be after her. Logic pointed to Eric as the intended victim. But who would want to kill Eric, and why? Was the gunman specifically out to get Eric? Would they try again? And who was this Jake Adams Eric seemed so suspicious of?

What concerned Jennie even more was that Gram was out there somewhere. Had she wandered off? Was she safe? Where was the rest of the family, and why hadn't they come to get her? Tomorrow she would get some answers. She had to. Donovan had said she could go to the crash site. Maybe she could persuade Eric to ride to this nearest neighbor with her—or at least give her directions. They might not have any answers, but they'd at least have a phone.

They might also have guns.

That reminder kept her awake for a long time.

9

Jennie awoke the next morning to the sound of chimes and a dull, persistent ache in the middle of her forehead. She felt dazed and confused. Why were there chimes playing? Slowly, the events of the days before unfurled. Gram. The plane crash. The night in the cave. This strange religious community. "Oh, God," she whimpered, "I don't want to be here. I want to go home. Why haven't Mom and Dad come for me?"

Someone knocked on her door.

"Go away." Jennie groaned, then rolled out of bed. "Jus-a-minute," she mumbled. She'd gotten halfway to the door when it opened.

Marilee poked her head in the door. "Good morning, Jennie. I see you're awake."

Jennie ran a hand through her tangled hair. "Not by choice."

"Lois told me to check on you. It's a good thing I did." Sounding far too perky and cheerful, she rambled on. "We'll be eating in ten minutes. You'll have to hurry."

Jennie rubbed her eyes. "What time is it?"

"Six-fifty."

A quick calculation indicated she'd slept only five hours. Definitely not enough. She'd read somewhere recently that teenagers required at least nine. Less than that resulted in sleep deprivation. Along with that came a bunch of problems like impaired judgment, poor grades, poor health. Jennie brushed aside that useless piece of information and focused back on Marilee, who was still going on about something.

"I thought you might need a clean dress. I hung one up near the shower. I can bring it in here if you want. Maybe you should eat first and shower later. Otherwise you'll be late."

"Marilee, will you shut up?" Jennie snapped. "I'm taking a shower."

"But—"

"I don't care if I'm late. What are they going to do? Kick me out?"

"I . . ." The girl seemed on the verge of tears. She backed out of the door. "I just didn't want you to miss breakfast."

Jennie covered her eyes and dragged her hands down her face. "I'm sorry. I shouldn't have gotten upset. I'm so tired and . . . I have a headache."

"I understand. I'm sure the headache will go away once you've eaten."

"I doubt that. It's probably from lack of sleep."

Marilee stiffened. "That's why we have rules. Early to bed, early to rise makes a man healthy, wealthy, and wise."

"Oh please." Jennie went back to sit on the bed. "I didn't exactly choose to get in late."

"Didn't you?" Marilee folded her arms and leaned against the doorpost. "You don't have to lie to me."

Jennie frowned. "What are you talking about? I'm not lying."

She sighed. "I saw you and Eric go out to the stables."

"So?"

"Nothing. Just don't expect me to feel sorry for you."

"Did you also know we were shot at?"

"Yes . . ." she hesitated. "But you shouldn't have been out there at that time of night."

Jennie was wide awake now and worried. Marilee liked Eric—a lot. Could jealousy have driven her to follow them out to the barn? Could she have been the one who fired at them? Marilee didn't seem the gun-toting type. Still, Jennie didn't quite trust her.

The chimes gave way to the dinner bell. Marilee unfolded her hands and reached for the doorknob. "You'd better hurry."

"Wait. I . . . I want my clothes."

"I told you, I hung a dress—"

"Not a dress. My own clothes. The ones I wore in here."

"We're not allowed to wear jeans here."

"I'm not staying. I have to search for my grandmother and find a way to contact my parents."

Marilee opened and closed her mouth. "I . . . you need to talk to Donovan—or Lois."

Jennie's heart hammered. "I can leave, can't I? I'm not a prisoner. Donovan said I could come and go as I please."

Marilee smiled. "Um . . . it isn't that easy. Of course you aren't forced to stay. It's just . . . look, I need to get to breakfast. You do too."

Jennie watched her walk down the hall. An uneasy feeling crept through her veins. They weren't going to let her leave. She'd read some things about cults. Once you got in, you didn't get out. Some brainwashed people. Was she being brainwashed?

Of course not. Donovan had said she could go out this morning to look for Gram. Would he change his mind? He had been reluctant to let her go. Eric had volunteered to go with her.

Eric. Was he going because he wanted to help, or to keep an eye on her?

Jennie stopped second-guessing herself and headed for the showers. "I'm leaving today." She made the statement aloud, as if hearing it herself could confirm it. "With or without your consent, Donovan, I'm getting out of here." If she couldn't get her own clothes, she'd do what she'd done last night—hitch up her skirt and make do.

Jennie showered and dressed, then took the time to braid her hair. She made it in to breakfast twenty minutes late. Several residents eyed her skeptically. Some cast her looks of disdain. Others smiled.

She ignored them and went to the buffet, only to find that the food had been taken away. Fine. Now she knew what happened when you were late. You didn't eat. She poured herself a glass of orange juice from the large container on the side bar, then found a seat at the nearest table.

She'd just gotten seated when Eric joined her. "Here." He set a plate in front of her. "Saved this for you."

Jennie's gaze met his and held it. "Thanks. You didn't have to."

"Yes, I did. If we're going to look for your grandmother, you need to eat. I don't want you fainting on me."

"We're going?"

"Yep." An easy grin spread across his face. "Donovan said we should. We can stay out as long as the weather holds up."

Jennie felt like hugging him. Instead, she thanked him and pushed her fork into the mound of scrambled eggs. Feeling a twinge of guilt at eating his food, she said, "What about you? Did you get enough to eat?"

He grinned. "Yeah. When I saw you weren't here, I asked Marilee. She said you'd be late, so I piled on some extra food." Jennie looked around the crowded room and spotted Marilee seated several tables away. Marilee tossed her a conspiratorial smile. Had she known Eric would save food for her? Jennie smiled back and turned her attention to her plate. Besides the eggs, there was sausage, which Eric explained wasn't sausage at all but a mix of soy, vegetables, and legumes. By the end of the meal, Jennie's mood had improved dramatically. She wasn't a prisoner after all. She and Eric were going to search for Gram. Her headache had disappeared, and her stomach was full.

When she got back to her room after breakfast, she

found Marilee bending over her bed. She jerked up as Jennie entered. "Oh, hi." She nodded toward the bed. "I hope you don't mind, but I made your bed and . . ."

Jennie's gaze drifted to the foot of the bed. "My clothes." Marilee had laid them out on the blanket. Jennie felt terrible about her earlier suspicions and the way she'd acted. "Thanks. That was really nice of you."

"I hope you find your grandmother." Marilee headed toward the door. "The Lord be with you."

Jennie thanked her again, and when the door closed, she stripped out of her dress and boots, then dragged on her jeans and turtleneck, topping it with her wool sweater. When she finished lacing up her hiking boots, Jennie grabbed her jacket and hurried down the hall through the common room and out the door. The gates stood open. Sun glistened on the freshly fallen snow. Beautiful morning. With renewed hope, Jennie broke into a run and didn't stop until she reached the barn.

"Hey," Eric greeted as he threw the saddle on Faith. "You look happy."

"I am. My headache's gone. I have my clothes back. The sun is shining, and we're going to find my grandmother."

Eric frowned. "We're going to look for clues. I can't promise we'll find her. Donovan said you shouldn't get your hopes up."

Jennie refused to let him dampen her spirits. "Do you need any help?"

"Nope." He tugged on the strap to adjust the saddle, then gave Faith a pat on the rear. "She's all set to go. Sable is already saddled."

They walked the horses out of the stables and into the sunlight. Faith seemed as eager as Jennie to get going. As Jennie mounted, she noticed Eric had placed saddlebags on both horses. Until then she hadn't given a thought to the supplies they might need. Not a good thing. If she had gone alone, she'd have been in trouble. "What's in the bags?"

"Food, emergency supplies, the usual. Out here you have to be prepared for anything."

"Um . . . thanks. I should have thought about that and given you a hand."

"No problem. Lois and I put it all together before breakfast." He grinned. "She even baked us a surprise treat for lunch. Wouldn't tell me what it was, but I have a hunch it's brownies. She makes them with cheesecake and raspberries swirled around inside."

Jennie's mouth watered. "Mmm. Sounds great. I have a good feeling about today." The comment was more wishful thinking than accurate. She knew all too well that the possibility of actually finding Gram was slim, and her intuition had her stomach tied in knots. Something told her not to go, but she wasn't about to listen. She had a chance to find Gram, and nothing could make her pass it up.

10

During the trek to the site of the plane crash, Jennie's suspicious mind drifted back to Marilee. What were her motives? Why had she been so nice to her? Marilee seemed almost too anxious to see her go. Was she planning something? An ambush? Suppose this was a trap to lure her away and then kill her.

Jennie shook her head. *You've been reading too many mysteries. Marilee is just a kindhearted Christian like Lois and Eric.*

The day was half gone by the time they reached the place where the downed plane should have been.

"I don't understand it." Jennie scanned the area, wishing she'd thought to get the GPS instrument back from Stan.

"It has to be here," Eric said. "Donovan said these co-ordinates would lead us right to it."

"Apparently he was wrong." Jennie leaned over to stroke Faith's neck. "Let's split up and circle around."

An hour later neither had found any trace of the plane or of Gram. Snow still covered the ground, but the body of the plane should have been easy to spot.

"Why don't we have lunch," Eric suggested as he dismounted. "We can look for it again."

Jennie agreed but didn't have much of an appetite. She was just finishing off her piece of brownie when she spotted a flash of light about two hundred yards from them—

the sun reflecting off a piece of metal. Her heart leaped to her throat. A gun? Was someone going to shoot at them again? Jennie shouted a warning to Eric, and they took cover behind some brush.

"There's no one there."

"I saw something. Look, there is it again." Jennie's hand went to her throat. "Maybe it's a piece of the plane."

"Let's check it out." They mounted their horses and rode over to take a look.

"It's a piece of the plane, all right." Jennie's gaze settled on the trees Gram had used to sheer the wings off. The broken branches bore witness to the crash.

"Where's the rest of it?" Eric spoke her thoughts.

Stunned, Jennie shaded her eyes from the sun. "I . . . I don't know. Unless . . ." Jennie had only one answer. "The authorities must have picked it up. You know, to determine the cause of the accident. Donovan might have been right when he suggested Gram had been rescued. They found the plane, picked her up, then came back to get the pieces."

"Maybe." Eric examined what looked like part of the wing. "But how could they move it so fast?"

"Good question. J.B. and my dad have connections with the federal government." She frowned. "Even if they got moving on it right away . . ." Jennie let her words trail off. The government wasn't known for its haste in any situation. But what other explanation could there be?

"It doesn't make sense." She slid her hand over the metal. "Why would they move the plane and not come for me?"

"Maybe the sheriff hasn't found them yet."

Jennie shook her head. "They'd call the authorities. I know they would."

"We might as well head back." Eric took hold of her arm. "There's nothing we can do here."

Jennie shrugged out of his grasp. "I can't go back. I have to get help. I have to find a phone or find the sheriff . . . or somebody." Looking out over the desolate landscape, she added, "Please, Eric. You have to help me. Take me to the Adams place."

"Are you crazy? We can't go there. I told you—"

"They don't like you, I know. But I'm one of them—" At Eric's injured expression, she said, "I don't hate you. But I'm not part of your group either."

It took a while, but Jennie finally convinced him to show her where the Adamses lived. He left her at the end of the long driveway, promising he'd wait. At first he'd insisted on going along, but Jennie wasn't certain what their reception would be. She felt she had a better chance at talking to them if she were alone.

Riding down the mile-long gravel road made Jennie feel alone and isolated. She was an easy target for anyone who might want her out of the way. *Not a rational thought,* Jennie told herself. No one wanted her dead—at least, not that she knew of. Marilee might be jealous, but she wasn't a killer. Jennie breathed a long sigh of relief when at last she neared the farmhouse. No one seemed to be around. There were no vehicles. An old tractor had been parked next to the barn some time ago. Dry grass reached the rusty old seat.

Jennie dismounted and tied Faith's reins to the split-rail fence surrounding the farmhouse. The hairs on the back of her neck stood at attention as she walked up the path to the front door. "Hello!" she called out. No one answered.

The porch creaked with each footstep Jennie made toward the door. Her heart raced. She called out again and knocked on the door. She didn't really expect an answer. The place had a deserted feel to it. She tried the door. Hinges squeaked as it swung inward. Taking a deep breath for confidence, Jennie stepped inside. Empty. They'd moved out.

"Well, you didn't come for a visit," she said aloud, her voice echoing across the wooden floors. "Find a phone."

In the living room, Jennie found a phone jack but no phone. Same in the kitchen. Determined, Jennie made her way up the stairs to the second floor. There were four bedrooms and a bath. All the doors were open but one. Jennie left it until last. No phones, not even a jack. She reached for the doorknob of the last room and hesitated. Her heart pounded in her throat. *There's nothing to be afraid of,* she told herself for the umpteenth time. *Nothing at all.*

She opened the door and caught sight of a mouse scurrying across the floor. Jennie yelped, then chuckled as the mouse's tiny feet slipped on the slick hardwood in its attempt to escape. "Relax." She let go of the knob and stepped inside. "I'm not going to hurt you."

But someone may hurt you. The thought thundered into her head just as she heard footsteps on the front porch. The front door squeaked open. The bedroom door behind her slammed shut.

Jennie dropped to the floor.

11

"Jennie!" a male voice drifted up the stairwell.

Eric? Jennie picked herself up off the floor and brushed off the dust. Embarrassed that she'd been so jumpy, she opened the door to the bedroom and stepped out into the hall. "I'm upstairs."

When no one answered, Jennie called again, "Eric?"

She descended the remaining stairs. An icy breeze swept through the open door. The hair on her arms and neck prickled. She had heard Eric. Hadn't she? Someone had definitely called her name. A creak sounded on the front porch again. Jennie's heart jumped to her throat.

A tall, grim-faced man in an oilskin coat appeared in the doorway. Jennie's fear drained into her rubbery legs when she recognized him. Stan, one of the men from the compound. But where was Eric? "What . . . what are you doing here?" she ventured.

Had Stan been the man who'd ambushed them before? Had he come back to finish the job? He'd had a weapon earlier.

"You okay?" Stan's voice was gravel rough, but his harsh gaze softened as he looked her over. "We thought we heard a gunshot."

"Oh." She tried to smile at the irony of it. "The wind must have caught the door upstairs. Where's Eric? I thought I heard him."

"You did." Stan glanced behind him. "I think he got

the wind knocked out of him. We both took cover." The corner of Stan's mouth twitched. "He did a belly flop off the porch."

Eric grunted as he pushed himself off the ground and straightened. "Not funny," he gasped.

A bubble of relief escaped Jennie's throat. "What are you guys doing here?" she repeated.

Eric mounted the steps, still brushing off the dust. "Stan came out to find us. He has news about your grandmother."

Jennie eyed him warily, looking for a sign. Good news or bad? She couldn't tell. "You found her?"

A grin broke out on Eric's face. "She's at the compound."

Jennie brushed past Stan and threw her arms around Eric. Tears welled in her eyes. "She's okay, then?" she asked as she stepped away.

"She's . . ." Eric glanced at Stan.

The big man nodded. "Your grandmother is alive, and the doctor says she'll be fine in a few days."

Jennie let out a huge sigh, tipped back her head, and offered up a prayer.

"I knew it would work out," Eric said smugly. "Things do if you just trust God."

"Let's go." Jennie jumped off the porch and headed toward her horse. "I want to see her."

Eric's gaze wandered from the house to the yard and the pastureland beyond. "Place looks deserted. Did you call—"

"No one's here. They've moved, I guess."

He frowned. "That's not possible." Eric stepped inside and looked around.

The blend of disbelief and anguish on his face took Jennie by surprise. "Eric, what's wrong?"

"I don't understand." Eric went inside, moving quickly from the kitchen to the living room. He started up the stairs and sank onto one of the steps halfway to the landing. Shaking his head, he murmured something Jennie couldn't understand.

"What's wrong?" Jennie followed him in and sat down beside him. "From the way you talked earlier, I'd have thought you'd be glad they've moved."

"Mom would never have moved without letting me know."

"Mom?" Jennie's mouth dropped open. "You . . . you live here? I thought—I mean . . . you were accusing these guys of shooting at us."

"My father and brother hated me for joining the Colony. Mom didn't want me to go either, but I think in a way she understood." He swept a hand over his face. "They wouldn't just leave like this. Something must have happened. Did you look around—in the barns and stuff?"

"No. Just the house. Everything's gone. Maybe they sent you a letter and it hasn't come."

"Eric." Stan's large form nearly filled the doorway. "We need to get back."

Jennie placed what she hoped was a comforting arm around Eric's shoulders. "I'm sorry."

"As am I," Stan said. "However, you left your family to follow the Lord. Have you changed your mind?"

Eric raised his head and abruptly stood. "No. But this isn't right. My mother would have told me."

"Perhaps I can locate them," Stan offered. "We can talk to Donovan when we get back."

Eric shook his head. "Don't bother. I lost my earthly family a long time ago. I have a new family now. I don't need them."

Stan nodded and, in a fatherly gesture, settled a hand on Eric's shoulder.

Jennie didn't know what to make of Eric's situation and reflected on it as they mounted their horses and headed back to the compound. Could his parents and brother really have turned their backs on Eric? She couldn't imagine anyone being that cruel.

Her own family wouldn't disown her no matter what she'd done. They loved one another. Jennie thought about the sacrifices her parents and grandparents had made over the years that reflected their unconditional love. Those thoughts brought her back to the nagging questions: *Where are your parents? Why haven't they come for you?*

Hurt bubbled up in her throat. Tears escaped their confines and trickled down her cheeks, turning bitter cold by the time they reached her jaw. She wiped them away with her jacket sleeve. Jennie couldn't imagine a snowstorm keeping her father from tracking her down. The only answer she could come up with was that her parents didn't know where she was. Which meant the authorities hadn't told them. Not possible, unless the authorities couldn't find them. *Or Donovan's men haven't told them.*

Jennie stared at the back of Stan's wide shoulders. Had he and the others lied about talking to the sheriff? There was something scary about him for sure. Yet, at the same time, she'd seen kindness in the way he comforted Eric. *Besides,* an inner voice told her, *he came all the way out here to tell you about Gram.*

She dug into her jacket pocket for a tissue and came up with only some lint.

"Here." Eric handed her a hanky. "What's wrong? I'd think you'd be happy, with your grandmother being found."

"I am—about that." Jennie explained how his family's being gone had started her thinking about her own parents. "They'd come for me as soon as they found out where I was." She pulled up on the reins to slow down and let Stan get ahead.

Eric slowed as well, giving her a what-are-you-doing look.

Jennie leaned toward him and whispered, "Makes me wonder if anyone told the authorities I was here."

"Of course they did." Eric seemed indignant. "Donovan wouldn't lie. Neither would Stan."

"How can you be sure? And how do you explain the fact that no one has tried to contact me?"

"It's only been two days. You didn't even know exactly where they were, and Bend is a pretty good-sized town."

"I know, but—"

"Trust God, Jennie. I've already given up my family to Him. I don't know where they are, but He does. Whatever is going on, I know God will take care of them—*and* me. Think about it, Jennie. He brought you *and* your grandmother safely to us."

Jennie sighed. "It's not that I don't believe in God and what He can do. I do. But God gave me a brain and instincts—we have to act on those sometimes. Faith is more than sitting around when there's a problem. It's also having the faith to do something about it."

"So what's the problem?"

"Something isn't right about all this. You said so yourself at your parents' farm. Don't you want to find out what happened to them?"

"Yes, but my job isn't to question God's will."

Jennie gritted her teeth. "Eric." Wanting to distance herself from Stan even more, she pulled back on the reins, bringing the horse to a stop.

Eric pulled up as well. "What are you doing?"

She nodded at Stan. "I didn't want him to overhear."

"Why?" Eric glanced at Stan, looking like a disobedient child. The man kept riding, head high, shoulders straight, reminding Jennie of a police officer on horse patrol. *An officer.* He carried himself like an authority. Could Stan be a government agent?

Eric grabbed her arm. "Jennie . . . why don't you want Stan to hear us?"

She tucked the random thoughts about Stan away for the time being and focused back on Eric. "I'm not sure I trust him."

"He's one of us." Eric shook his head, clearly annoyed at her suggestions.

"That doesn't make him a good person."

As if knowing they were talking about him, Stan stopped and twisted around in his saddle and shouted, "Everything okay back there?"

"Fine," Jennie yelled back. "We . . . we were just talking."

Jennie urged Faith forward. Stan turned back around and resumed his previous pace, staying well ahead of them.

"Anyway, that's not what I wanted to talk to you about," Jennie said, going back to her earlier concerns. "It's your parents. You keep talking about God's will. Well, what if this isn't God's will that they're gone? What if it's someone else's?"

Deep furrows etched Eric's forehead. "What's your point?"

"You said there were outsiders around here who hated the Colony and that they'd killed two of your members."

"Right. So what does that have to do with my family?"

"I'm not sure, but if the killers murdered the two men just because they were members of the Colony, maybe they also hate the families of people at the Colony. Think of Hitler and how he exterminated the Jews."

"You're saying they might have killed my parents and brother because I joined the Colony?"

"Maybe not entirely. But what if your family refused to be a part of their vigilante group or tried to fight them? Maybe they knew something or had evidence."

"I don't know, Jennie. That seems pretty farfetched."

"I'm sure your parents didn't stop loving you when you joined the Colony. They were probably hurt and angry, but—"

"Dad disowned me. He said he would if I joined, and he did. My brother wouldn't even talk to me. When I left, he wouldn't even say good-bye."

"They were hurt. Maybe your dad thought that threatening you would make you change your mind. People say and do things they don't mean when they're hurt."

"Doesn't matter. They've moved and didn't tell me, which proves they don't care. God is my Father. The people at the Colony are my brothers and sisters."

"Okay, but aren't you curious as to what really happened?"

"Yeah, but what can I do about it?"

Jennie shrugged. "I thought maybe you and I could go back to your parents' ranch tomorrow and have another look around."

"What good would that do?"

Before Jennie could respond, Eric urged Sable forward. "Stan, wait up."

Jennie dug her heels into Faith's side a little harder than she needed to. She waited in anticipation for Eric to tell Stan about her crazy theories, but he didn't. Apparently he didn't feel they were worth mentioning. Fine. If Eric didn't want to go, maybe she'd go by herself. She couldn't let it go. It just wasn't in her nature.

It took forty minutes to ride from the ranch to the compound. The last twenty were painfully silent. Stan and Eric both looked like they carried heavy loads. Once they arrived, Stan turned to Eric. "I'll take care of the horses for you. I imagine you'd like to take Jennie in to see her grandmother."

"Sure." Eric didn't seem all that enthused.

"I can go in alone," she said.

"I'd like to see her too." Eric's gaze slid to meet hers, offering what Jennie saw as a private apology.

Jennie nodded and they set off. Marilee and Lois greeted them as they came through the main gate a couple minutes later.

"Isn't it wonderful?" Marilee clasped her hands and did a little dance. "The Lord has answered our prayers. He brought her nearly to our doorstep. One of the men found her in the stable. Didn't I tell you everything would work out?"

Jennie smiled. Part of her felt like dancing too, but something in the older woman's demeanor held her back.

"Jennie." Lois fell into step with the others. "Before you see your grandmother, there's something you should know."

"What's wrong? Stan said she was alive."

"She is." Lois hesitated. "But she's very ill. She's suffered a head injury, as you know. She also has a broken arm. She looks—"

"But she'll be okay, right? Stan said she'd be okay."

"The doctor seems to think so." She smiled and patted Jennie's hand. "I'm sure she'll be fine. I just didn't want you to be alarmed."

Marilee kept talking to Eric and Lois about the miracle. They in turn raved about God's perfect timing. Jennie tuned them out. Her head and her heart hurt with the anticipation of seeing Gram, especially after Lois's warning.

Her heart quickened as they reached their destination. The building was much like the others, Jennie noted as they reached it. A cross graced the entry, and a sign posted to the right of the door read *Hospital*. They walked into an open area that seemed to serve several purposes. There were chairs making up a waiting area to the right. Two small, round tables sat next to a cupboard holding drink containers and what looked like snacks.

To the left was a small chapel with two small stained-glass windows. One showed Christ carrying the cross. The other was of Christ risen, arms outstretched. From burden to hope. Jennie felt the burden deeply now. *Gram will be okay,* she reminded herself. She forced herself to look at the resurrection. *Please, God, let her be all right.*

"She's in here." Lois led them into a large ward behind the double doors. The smell of industrial-strength room deodorizer tried to hide the distinct smell of incontinency.

"It smells like a nursing home," Jennie murmured.

"In a way, it is," Lois said. "This is where our elderly

and frail come when they're sick or dying."

Four of the beds were occupied by patients who fit Lois's description of elderly. All had white hair that blended in with the room itself. Jennie let her gaze wander over the clean white walls and ceiling. Six beds with white sheets and spreads lined each side of the room, dormitory style. Each bed sat in front of a window with white shades and curtains. Those on the south side were drawn to keep out the late-afternoon sun. A woman in a long blue dress and white apron walked toward them. Most modern nurses wore scrubs and uniforms in all different colors. Though Jennie had seen pictures of nurses in hats, she'd never actually met one.

"Hello," the nurse said as she approached. "I'm Kimberly. You must be Jennie."

Jennie nodded. "Where's Gram?"

Kimberly's gaze flickered over Eric, Lois, and Marilee in a warm greeting before settling back on Jennie. "Behind those curtains." She pointed to the last bed on the right. "We felt she needed the privacy." Her smile faded. "You can see her, but only for a few minutes. She needs to rest as much as possible." Looking at the others, she said, "I'd like you to wait out here. The doctor said we needed to limit visitors."

Jennie followed Kimberly back to the last bed on the left. The curtains opened, and Jennie slipped inside. Her heart dropped to her feet. Stan had warned her. So had Lois. Jennie sucked in a deep breath and let it out slowly. Nothing could have prepared her for this.

12

A baseball-sized lump clogged Jennie's throat. She swallowed hard and moved forward until she reached the side rail. *There's been a mistake. This isn't Gram. It can't be.*

The still, pale woman lying against the stark white bedding bore little resemblance to Helen Bradley. Gram was vibrant and active—a spy, a writer, and a strong, independent woman. Gram was young—at least she seemed so to Jennie. She wasn't at all like Grandma Calhoun, who'd been old forever. Not that being old was a bad thing. She'd loved Grandie too.

The woman in the bed looked older than Gram by at least ten years. Her short salt-and-pepper hair stuck out at all angles. Gram's face was pretty—deep blue eyes like Jennie's, and fair skin. Now multicolored bruises covered half her face. A bandage covered the place on her forehead that had been bleeding. Even as the denials came and went, Jennie knew the truth. This was Gram. No mistake.

An anguished cry escaped Jennie's lips. It didn't seem possible, but she looked worse than when Jennie had left her at the crash site. An IV dripped fluid into a vein on her left hand. A cast covered Gram's right arm from the knuckles to about four inches above the elbow. Her breathing seemed labored and shallow.

Glazed and unfocused, Gram's eyes opened for a moment, then closed again.

"Gram, I'm here."

Jennie grasped the fingers of Gram's left hand.

Gram moaned. Her face contorted in pain.

Jennie let go and grabbed the rail. "I'm so sorry. I didn't mean to hurt you."

"I don't think you hurt her." Though the voice sounded tender and filled with compassion, it startled Jennie.

She spun around, nearly knocking over a pitcher of water on the bedside table. "You scared me. What—where did you come from?"

Donovan smiled. "I've been here since they brought her in. Praying. You were so intent on your grandmother you must not have noticed."

"No, I didn't."

"As I was saying, I don't believe you hurt her. She's in a great deal of pain."

"Why don't they give her something?"

"They have, my dear. The nurse medicated her just before you arrived."

"Oh."

"Why don't you sit here beside me. You look a little unsteady."

Jennie felt unsteady. "Thanks," she managed. "I'm okay." She didn't want to leave Gram's side, but after a few minutes she caved in and eased into the straight-backed wooden chair.

After several more long and silent minutes, she got up again. Donovan made her nervous. Not him exactly. His silence. Since offering her the chair, he'd been so quiet she wondered from time to time if he was even breathing. He just sat there, praying or meditating. At least that's what she assumed he was doing. With bowed head he had a reverent, priestly look about him. Jennie didn't want silence. She wanted answers.

Disturbing him didn't seem right. Still . . . She cleared her throat. "Donovan."

He looked up, his gaze forgiving. "Yes?"

"I . . . I need to know what happened. How did you find her, and . . ." Jennie hesitated, almost afraid to ask. "Why is she here? Shouldn't she be in a real hospital?"

"This is a real hospital and the best place for her right now. We have a qualified staff seeing to her needs." Donovan held up his hand to quiet Jennie's protest. "She came to us. Apparently walked in during the night or this morning. Stan found her in the stables."

Jennie rubbed her forehead. "Where? Eric and I were there—we didn't see her."

"Stan found her shortly after you left. She had apparently tucked herself into a corner of the stall away from the door to keep warm."

"I can't believe I didn't see her. I should have known she was there."

"Nonsense. How could you?" He placed a hand on her forearm. "There is no reason to feel guilty. Just be happy she was found. Praise be to God for the miracle of her life. I don't know how she managed—angels, most likely. Considering her condition, the odds were against it. We were all surprised." He placed both hands on his knees and stood. "I suppose we shouldn't be. God does work in mysterious ways."

"Yes, but . . ." Jennie wished she could simply thank God, but it didn't seem that simple. She couldn't get over the feeling that things weren't as they seemed. Jennie had no idea what was out of place. She only knew that something wasn't right.

"Would you like to meet Dr. Paul? Perhaps he can put your mind at ease."

Jennie nodded and followed Donovan through the ward. At the center, he turned at the nurses' station and stopped at a closed door. After tapping lightly and receiving a "come in" from inside, he opened the door and stepped into the room. It was an office, actually, with a desk and file cabinet.

"Paul," Donovan greeted the balding man with glasses

perched on his nose and feet resting on the desk. He wore a white lab coat over khaki pants and a white shirt.

"Donovan. Come in." He placed the book he'd been reading on the desk and swung his feet down.

Donovan introduced Jennie. "I'll leave you two to talk. Jennie has some questions about her grandmother's condition."

"Fine. I'll be happy to talk with her."

Donovan eased out and closed the door behind him.

"Please, have a seat." Dr. Paul gestured toward the chair behind her. Jennie dropped onto it and questions spilled out. "Why is she here? What are you doing for her? How badly is she hurt?"

While she talked, the doctor reached behind him for a cup, filled it with juice, and handed it to her.

Jennie took it and set it on the desk. "Please. Just answer my questions."

He did. Calmly and gently, as Donovan had, the doctor explained Gram's condition. It was nothing the others hadn't already told her or that she hadn't seen for herself, but hearing him talk in a professional way calmed her. "Her vitals are good . . . blood pressure, heart. Her condition is guarded but certainly not life-threatening. She's exhausted, and it will take several days for her to regain her strength."

As he continued to explain, Jennie drank the juice, and when he finished, she asked for another glass. "I'm really thirsty."

"Let me get you some water, then." He smiled back at her over his shoulder while he filled her glass.

Jennie greedily downed the water. "So, doc . . ." Jennie set the glass back on the desk and leaned lazily back in her chair. She felt comfortable now with Dr. Paul and Gram's care. Maybe he could help with another matter. "What if she gets worse and needs emergency care? Could you lifeflight her into Bend or Portland?"

"We'd get her the best medical care possible. However, she's not in danger, Jennie."

"I know. I believe you. I'm just thinking that if you had an emergency, you could call for help. You could fly her out."

"Yes, I suppose we could."

"Then why can't you pull some strings and find a way to call my parents?"

"Pardon me?" His forehead knitted in a frown.

"I need to talk to them, let them know I'm here so they can come get me."

"I'm sure the authorities have been notified."

"Then why haven't I heard from them? Why haven't they come?"

"I'm afraid I can't answer that. If the authorities have been contacted, I'm sure they're doing their best to locate your family."

"They're not that hard to find. They'd be looking for me too. I don't understand."

"I'm sorry this is distressing you. Perhaps the Lord has a reason for delaying your departure from us. One obvious reason is your grandmother."

"What do you mean?"

"She needs you. She may not even know you're here at the moment, but her recovery will be much faster if she has family with her."

"We'd take her with us."

"Moving her now would be very hard on her."

Jennie tucked her hair behind her ear. "I want to go home."

"Of course you do," Dr. Paul soothed. "That's understandable. You miss your family. I'll talk to Donovan. Perhaps he's had some news. Meanwhile, why don't you get some rest. You look like you're ready to collapse yourself."

"No, I don't—"

"Tell you what." Dr. Paul stood. "You can sleep here, right next to your grandmother. How would that be?"

Jennie could think of no reason whatsoever to disagree. She did need a nap, and being close to Gram . . . yes.

Dr. Paul led her out to the main area, where he signaled the nurse.

The room swayed. In slow motion, the nurse moved toward them. Jennie heard Dr. Paul say, "Help me get her into bed."

Jennie's eyes closed. Her knees buckled. Darkness folded around her like a blanket.

She came to for a moment when the nurse touched a cool hand to her wrist to check her pulse. *The juice. Dr. Paul put something in my juice.* The vague and disjointed revelation drifted in just before darkness fell again.

13

Jennie awoke to the sound of a bell and the smell of food. Silverware clinked.

"I'm sorry to wake you." Kimberly, the nurse she'd met earlier, touched her shoulder. "It's dinnertime, and I'm sure you must be hungry."

Jennie rubbed her eyes and yawned. "Thanks." She swung her legs over the edge of the bed. Her head throbbed. Again. *The juice.*

"My head hurts," she told the nurse. "It hurts every time I wake up. Um . . . I think it's the juice. What do you people put in that stuff, anyway?" As soon as she'd said it, she wished she hadn't. At the moment it didn't seem wise to trust anyone here—not even the nurse or the doctor.

"Our juice?" She frowned. "Hmm. It's made with all-natural products. Mainly a combination of fruits and herbs. You could be allergic to one of the herbs. It happens sometimes. I'll tell Dr. Paul."

"No, don't bother. The headaches aren't that bad. They go away after I eat."

Kimberly nodded. "Well, if they persist, tell us. We can alter the formula for you once we find out what you're sensitive to."

"I won't be around here long enough for that." *Besides,* Jennie added to herself, *I don't plan on drinking any more of it.* "How's Gram?" she asked, changing the subject. The curtains around Gram's bed had been pushed back, and she looked to be sleeping.

"About the same. We're hoping to see some improvement by morning."

"I hope so."

Jennie sat on a nearby chair to put on her boots. Kimberly and Dr. Paul must have taken them off when they put her to bed. Before leaving, she kissed Gram. "Get better. I'll be by later. I love you." This time when Jennie took Gram's hand, there was a slight pressure. Gram knew she was there. That thought nearly took away the headache and the grogginess still fogging her brain.

On her walk across the compound, Jennie mulled over the suspicions she had about the juice. Kimberly had suggested a sensitivity to herbs. Jennie wasn't convinced. She'd been offered juice by Donovan and the doctor when she'd been upset. Each time she'd come away feeling less anxious and more tired. Had they been putting something extra in her drink?

She made it to the dining room just as the residents were standing to offer thanks. Slipping into the vacant spot beside Eric, Jennie folded her hands and bowed her head. At the end of the table blessing, as they went through the buffet line, she offered a silent prayer of her own. *Thank you, God, for bringing Gram here. Please make her better so we can leave. And please help us to get out—and to find out what happened to Eric's family. Amen.*

"Mmm," Eric licked his lips. "Spaghetti, my favorite." He piled on noodles and a rich red tomato sauce with what looked like ground beef. Another meat substitute. This time she didn't ask.

"Looks good." Jennie's stomach felt as if it had been neglected for a week. She took an ample portion of the main course, a serving of green beans, a tossed green salad, and a buttery slice of garlic bread. When they came to the drinks, Eric poured himself a large glass of juice. Jennie took water.

"How's your grandmother?" Eric asked as they sat down. "You were gone a long time."

"The same. I talked to Dr. Paul." *He drugged me. Gave me something that knocked me out.* As much as she wanted to tell Eric, she couldn't. Not here. Not yet. Maybe later when they were alone, though she didn't think it would do much good. She doubted he'd believe her.

"Here you are, my dear." The woman seated next to Jennie handed her a glass of juice. "I noticed you forgot yours."

I didn't forget. Jennie held back the caustic reply. Instead, she answered with a polite, "Thank you, but I wasn't going to have any with dinner."

"Oh." The woman cast her a look of concern. "You must."

Several other table mates glanced over at her, nodding in agreement.

"Why?" Jennie tried to keep the annoyance she felt out of her voice.

"For your health and well-being," her table mate explained. "It's like a multivitamin—has all our basic requirements. Vitamins, minerals, different herbs . . ."

"Is there some kind of rule that says you have to drink it?"

The woman beside her smiled. "No rule. Just a recommendation. A tradition, really. I started drinking it forty years ago. Three times a day without fail. Keeps me going strong. I'm eighty-two, you know."

Jennie didn't know. The woman did look healthy—wrinkled as a raisin, but healthy.

"It's wonderful for your complexion too."

Jennie offered what she hoped was a genuine smile. "You've convinced me. But if it's okay, I'll wait and drink it after dinner. I don't usually have juice and spaghetti together."

"Of course." The woman, who then introduced herself as Dory, seemed sincerely concerned. Jennie doubted

Dory or any of the others knew what she knew. Or thought she did. The juice was tainted—at least hers seemed to be. Or was it? Except for that first day when Marilee had brought juice to her room, it had come from a common pitcher. If it was tainted, wouldn't everyone be affected? None of these people showed signs of being drugged.

Maybe it's just what they say it is. They freely admitted there were additives—vitamins, minerals, herbs. Maybe the nurse was right, that Jennie had a sensitivity or allergy to one of them. Still, she had no intention of drinking it. Maybe she could find a potted plant somewhere, or just flush it down the toilet. On the other hand, maybe only the drinks she'd gotten from Donovan and Dr. Paul had been drugged.

By the end of the meal, she'd talked herself out of her paranoia and downed the juice. However, she was still harboring suspicions about Donovan and Dr. Paul.

Three hours later, Jennie suffered no ill effects of the juice she'd had at dinner. In fact, her headache had cleared and she felt refreshed, which made her even more suspicious of Donovan and the doctor. After the evening service Jennie opted out of the fellowship time and hurried across the courtyard to the hospital.

When Jennie reached the halfway mark, she heard someone running behind her. She spun around, fear rising in her throat when she saw a dark figure crouching in the shadows, making his way toward her.

"Jennie," came a hoarse whisper. "Wait up."

When the shadowy figure passed a lighted window, her fear shrank. "Eric, what—"

"Shh." He grabbed her arm and pulled her into the shadows of a building. "Keep it down," he whispered. "I need to talk to you."

"Why all the secrecy? What's going on?"

"I got to thinking about what you said when we were at the farm. I want to go back, have a look around. I'm heading out tonight and wondered if you wanted to go with me."

"Right now?"

"As soon as we can get ready." He glanced around. "Will you come with me?"

"Of course."

He hugged her to him. "I knew I could count on you. The horses are set to go." His dark gaze met hers as he started to move away.

Jennie's breath caught at the expression on his face. He closed the distance between them and kissed her. Eric released her and stepped back. He seemed embarrassed and unsure. "I'm sorry."

Jennie couldn't help but smile. "Don't be." Now it was her turn to be embarrassed. She glanced toward the hospital. "I was just going to see my grandmother."

Eric nodded. "I'll wait here for you."

Jennie ran the rest of the way to the hospital. She felt a bit guilty at her short stay, but she knew Gram would understand. Maybe now she'd finally get some answers.

Within ten minutes, Jennie was back at the building where she'd met Eric earlier.

"How is she?"

"No change."

"I'm still praying."

"Thanks. I am too. She'll be okay. Gram's tough." It had taken enormous strength and endurance to get to the compound. Would she have enough left to get well? Jennie pushed the worry from her mind. She had to be strong enough for both of them.

She followed Eric back to the common room between the two dorms and into the kitchen. They were taking the tunnel to the stables. "I take it no one here knows what we're doing."

"I didn't want them to know. This is a weakness on my part. Donovan would have let me go, but he'd have sent one of the men along. I need to do this myself." He opened the cupboard door and pulled out the back panel. Handing Jennie the flashlight, he motioned her to go ahead. Once inside the tunnel, Jennie turned and shone the light on him so he could see to properly close the doors.

"Why are you bringing me?" she asked when they moved on.

"You're smart. You notice things." He draped an arm around her shoulder and took the flashlight back. "You're objective. And you're right."

"What do you mean?"

"About things not being quite right here. I've felt that, too, but never wanted to question it."

"You think Donovan or someone here might have something to do with your parents' and brother's disappearance?" Jennie ducked under a cobweb. "Or those deaths?"

"No." He shook his head. "Not like that. I was talking about their philosophy. They are good and kind people and wouldn't hurt anyone."

Jennie wasn't certain about that but didn't voice her opinion. She didn't trust any of them. Except Eric and maybe Lois. Jennie heard a thud and then a faint moan.

Eric stopped her. "Listen."

She swallowed hard, peering into the darkness ahead of them. "I heard it. Sounded almost like someone fell."

"It came from over there." Eric lifted the light higher. They moved forward. The beam hit the closed passageway she'd seen on the last trip through there.

"I don't hear anything now." He shrugged. "Probably just some of the wood settling."

"Sounded human to me."

"Wood can do that."

They moved ahead, but Jennie kept glancing behind. Secret passageways, locked doors . . . What she'd heard hadn't been wood groaning. She wanted to see what lay beyond the locked door. Tomorrow she'd ask Eric or Lois to take her through the tunnels on the other side.

14

"Ow." Jennie slid off her horse and rubbed her sore rear. "I've ridden more since I got here than I have in my entire life. Getting lost didn't help."

"We didn't get lost." Eric dismounted and grabbed the reins of both horses. "Just took me a while to get my bearings."

"I know," Jennie sympathized. She really couldn't fault him. It had taken over an hour to reach the farmhouse where Eric had grown up. They'd ridden most of the way in intense silence, straining to see the trail and maintain the right direction in the nearly black night. The moon and stars occasionally peeked through the velvet cloud cover, giving them brief moments of clarity.

Snow crunched beneath Jennie's booted feet. Moonlight glistened on the snow-covered ground, lighting their destination.

"Let's put the horses in the barn," Eric said. "They'll be warmer there, and it'll be easier to feed and water them." Puffs of steam escaped his lips as he talked.

Jennie stuffed her cold hands into her pockets. She could use a little warmth too. Her gloves and ski jacket had helped but didn't stop the bone-chilling cold from seeping through to her skin. She followed him to the building nearest the house. As they entered, a horse whinnied from a far stall.

"What. . . ?" Eric handed Jennie the reins and raced

back to where the sound had come from. Beams from the flashlight bounced around the barn. The mystery horse whinnied again.

"Eric?"

"Come on back, Jennie. You're not going to believe this."

Following the light, Jennie made her way to the back of the barn. There in the stall was a mare nursing a foal. "Oh, he's so cute." She leaned in for a better look.

"This isn't right," he mumbled. He unlatched the gate and went in. "Mom and Dad would never go off and leave a horse in labor." He stroked the horse's sleek black neck. "Not unless something forced them out."

"Maybe they didn't know she was here."

"They knew. Otherwise she'd be pastured. Someone put her in here." Eric hung the flashlight from a high nail nearby. "The colt can't be more than two or three days old—which means they were here then." Pointing behind Jennie, Eric said, "There's still some grain in the bin. Grab those buckets on the wall and start feeding the horses. I'll get some water."

Jennie doled out feed to all three horses, taking extra time to pet the colt and its mother. After taking care of the horses, Jennie and Eric began their search of the house.

"I don't understand any of this," Eric told Jennie as he opened the coat closet in the entry. He ran his hand across the shelf, scattering a layer of dust. It was as empty as the living room. Stripped bare. "Mom wouldn't have left the place without cleaning it up."

"Maybe this vigilante group you've been talking about threatened them." Jennie moved into the kitchen and started opening cupboards, shining the flashlight into each. "They got scared and ran, then hired a moving company to pack things up."

"My dad wouldn't run."

"Not even to save his family?"

Eric lifted himself onto the counter near the sink. "I'm

worried, Jen. I'm sure they didn't leave on their own. They were forced out. Maybe taken out to the pasture and killed."

"Don't even say that. If someone wanted to kill them, why would they bother moving all the furniture?"

"Because they didn't want anyone to be suspicious. They wanted it to look like my folks moved out."

"Is there any possibility there's something here they'd want and had to get rid of your parents to get it?"

"I can't think of anything . . . except maybe the property itself. But if anything happened to my parents, I'd inherit the place."

"At least we know they didn't move out on their own. They were forced. We have to find out who did this."

"I just thought of something." Jennie closed the pantry door. "You said you'd inherit, but would you really? Marilee told me that when you join the order, everything you own is turned over to the community."

"Yeah. I signed over my worldly belongings, but . . . Hey, I know where you're going with this, and it won't work. If you're implying that Donovan got rid of my parents, you're crazy. He'd never hurt anyone. Besides, we don't need money. We make plenty from the products we sell."

"Property. Your parents' property borders—"

"I know," he answered angrily. "But the Colony doesn't need more property. We have plenty."

"Okay," Jennie said. "Calm down. I'm just thinking about possibilities. Whoever forced your parents out and emptied the place had a motive."

"They knew too much. Suppose Dad or Jake found out what the other ranchers were up to—that they were going to destroy the Desert Colony. He might have threatened to go to the authorities."

"Yesterday you were practically accusing them of shooting at us."

"I was angry and frustrated. Lois said Jake was a

suspect. I didn't know what to believe. I just know they wouldn't kill anyone."

"I hope you're right. Let's finish searching the house for clues, then check the other buildings."

"What are we looking for?" Eric jumped off the counter.

"I have no idea. Hopefully we'll know when we find it."

Fifteen minutes later Eric and Jennie left the house. The movers, whoever they were, had been thorough. Nothing was left—no evidence that Eric and his family had ever lived there.

Eric led the way to the farthest building. "Machine shop," he answered when Jennie asked what it was. "We store some of the farm equipment in there. Dad has a workshop in it too. He could fix just about everything." He cleared his throat and turned away, but not before Jennie saw his tears.

"Eric, I'm sorry . . ." Jennie reached toward him, but he moved on, apparently not wanting to be consoled.

They walked across a pad of concrete and past an old-style gas pump that sat at the side of the building. Weeds had grown up between the cracks. Two double-wide garage doors nearly covered the front. Eric approached the building from the side near the gas tank and opened a smaller door.

Hinges squeaked. Eric held the door until Jennie got in, then let it go. It shut with another screech and a thud. The room smelled like a grimy old garage—grease, oil, gas. Eric directed the light across a cracked concrete floor that was covered with dirt and grime. The beam traveled up, revealing a green John Deere tractor parked in front of the first door. Behind it was an antique yellow truck partially dismantled.

"Dad's hobby. He loved this old beater."

The flashlight revealed a wall covered with tools, shelves, and a work counter. "Looks like they forgot about this stuff," Eric mused. "Dad wouldn't have left it."

"Or they haven't finish loading." Jennie pointed to the moving truck parked in front of the other set of overhead garage doors. She inched forward, not wanting to think what it meant.

"They weren't being moved anywhere." Eric's voice had gone flat. He pulled a hand through his hair and leaned against the truck. "They're dead."

"We don't know that for sure." Jennie took the flashlight out of his limp hand. "Come on. Let's keep looking."

"I've seen enough."

"Fine. Stay here. I'm going to look inside."

Jennie went around to the front of the moving truck and slid behind the wheel. The keys were in the ignition. She leaned over and opened the glove box.

"What are you doing?" Eric opened the passenger-side door.

"When you rent a truck, you have to sign papers. I thought maybe there'd be something to tell us who did it. Unfortunately, there's nothing except the manual."

"They probably stole it."

"Let's look in the back." Jennie hopped down and went around to the back. Eric was already sliding open the back panel.

Neither spoke as the light flashed over what had been in the house. Mattresses, chairs, a television set, a bookshelf, pots and pans. Though there were a few boxes, most items had been thrown in haphazardly. Eric pulled the door down and sat on the bumper, then rested his head in his hands.

Jennie sat next to him and found it hard to imagine what he must be going through. Seeing the empty house had shaken him up. But seeing the furniture, the pans his mother had used to cook with, the furniture they'd sprawled out on to watch TV or talk . . . Jennie tipped the flashlight back and forth around the shed, then stopped abruptly as the light caught something red partly hidden under a large tarp. It looked like part of—

"Listen." Eric grabbed the flashlight and snapped it off.

"What are you doing?" Panic welled in her chest like a surging wave.

"Shh. Just listen."

The roar of a vehicle sent Jennie's heart skittering. Headlights flashed into the garage door windows and the cracks between the aged wooden walls.

"They've come back to finish the job." Eric stepped in front of her. "I won't let them."

"Wait!" Jennie grabbed for him, hitting only air. She caught him at the side door. "Don't go out there."

Eric pushed her aside. "Get out of here. Try to get to the barn. There's another door in the back. Ride back to the Colony and tell them we need help."

Jennie had no intention of leaving him. Eric had taken only a few steps out of the shed when the lights from a truck caught him. He stopped, glanced Jennie's way, and started to run back. A gunshot exploded and Eric fell.

15

"Eric!" Jennie screamed as he fell at her feet. She grabbed his jacket and pulled him inside, then shut the door and bolted it.

"Oh, dear God, let him be okay." The panic in her chest swelled. Her breaths came in short gasps. Someone pounded on the door, and she heard hard, angry voices. "Open up."

Something hard smashed against the door.

Eric. She had to focus on Eric. Jennie dragged him away from the door and under the work counter, hopefully out of sight. *Think, McGrady, think.*

"Forget him," one of the men roared. "We've got work to do."

Work? What did they mean? Were they coming inside?

Eric groaned. "They shot me. They actually shot me."

"I know. Where?"

"Shoulder." He grasped his left arm and tried to sit. "Hurts."

"Hold still." Jennie reached inside his jacket. Warm blood oozed around her fingers and dripped across the back of her hand. "I have to stop the bleeding."

"No point." Eric struggled to sit up. "They're going to kill us both."

"You said there was another door." She put an arm around his waist. "Come on. Lean on me. We can make it."

"You get the back," one of the men yelled. "Douse it good."

Jennie froze. The strong, sickening smell of gasoline seeped through the shed's old boards, leaving no doubt as to their intention. They hadn't forgotten the tools. And they hadn't come back to get the moving truck. They were going to torch the place.

In seconds, flames surrounded the old building. Once the fire caught the petroleum products on the floor and in the vehicles, the whole place would explode.

"Come on. We have to get out of here. Now!" Jennie pulled Eric to his feet, and the two of them stumbled across the floor, away from the grease.

"It's no use." Eric grimaced. "Leave me."

"No way. Work with me, Eric. I have an idea." Jennie pushed Eric into the passenger seat of the moving truck, then raced around and jumped into the cab. In an automatic motion she belted herself in and turned the key. The truck lurched.

"The clutch." Eric grimaced and held his shoulder. "Step on the clutch." He grabbed his seat belt and clicked the buckle into place.

Jennie slammed her foot against the clutch and twisted the key again. This time the engine came to life. Flames covered the entire wall in front of her now. The old timbers melted in the intense heat.

Jennie's hand closed around the shift stick. She had two choices: Go straight ahead through the back wall or back out through the metal garage door. Straight ahead, she decided. Gears ground as she pushed the stick forward. "I can't." She bit her lip until she drew blood. "It won't go into gear."

"Here." Eric leaned over. Pushing her hand away, he grabbed the stick and maneuvered it around, pushing it into first.

Jennie let up on the clutch and depressed the gas pedal. The truck jumped forward and died.

God, please. Jennie held her breath and tried again. Flames lapped at the sides of the truck. In moments the fire would find the gas tank. Jennie pressed steadily on the gas pedal. The truck moved slowly at first, then shot forward as Jennie gave it more gas.

"We made it!" Jennie cheered as they shot through the flaming wall. The ride was bumpy with the truck going over the rough terrain. But they were clear of the fire and hopefully clear of the men who meant to kill them.

"Jennie, look out!" Eric braced himself as the truck rammed into a fence post and shot into a watering hole.

She slammed on the brake, and the truck shuddered to a stop.

Jennie closed her eyes and dropped her head back against the seat. Her hands still gripped the steering wheel.

"You did it, Jen." Eric reached across the seat to hug her. "I didn't think we'd make it."

"I wasn't so sure, either, for a while." In the rearview mirror Jennie could see the entire shop engulfed in flames, burning white hot against the dark sky.

"We're not out of this yet," she cautioned. "Those guys are probably going to come after us. They meant to get rid of everything in the shop—including us and this truck."

"We'd better run. They won't find us out there." Eric climbed out of the truck and, after stumbling several feet, dropped to the ground.

Jennie pried her fingers off the steering wheel and slid across the seat. For those few terrifying moments, she'd forgotten about his injury. She jumped down and almost fell, her legs so rubbery she had to hold on to the side of the truck to steady herself. Water from the shallow pond seeped into her boots. Three steps and she was free of the water. She hunkered down beside him.

"They're leaving." Eric pointed to the left of the shop, where taillights headed out of the driveway and out to the main road.

Relieved, Jennie knelt down next to Eric. "How's the shoulder?"

"Still hurts. Need to get back and stop the fire from spreading." He struggled to get up again.

"It's too late. There's nothing we can do."

"The barn . . . the horses. If the fire jumps . . ."

He didn't have to finish. Jennie's uncertain gaze darted from Eric to the barn.

"I'm okay." He gripped his arm again and got up. "Let's go."

An explosion rocked the night, sending a fiery plume high into the night sky. "The gas tank," Jennie guessed. Several more explosions came after that. Eric's dad's vintage truck. The tractor. Jennie watched in horror as flames from the machine shop shot out like fireworks. Burning debris landed on the roof of the barn. Jennie broke into a run, leaving Eric behind.

By the time she reached the barn, the fire had taken hold. Sable and Faith whinnied and pranced in circles. Staying low, Jennie quickly untied them and led them toward the open barn door. Sable reared and broke into a run. Faith followed.

The roof of the barn where the fire had started was already beginning to cave in. Smoke had filled the barn, making it hard to breathe. Coughing, Jennie brought up the neck of her T-shirt and covered her nose and mouth, then bolted for the far stall, where the mare and foal stood. She opened the door, but the mare wouldn't budge. "Come, on girl. We have to get you out of here."

In response, the mare lifted her front legs, pawing at Jennie. Jennie ran around to the other side of the stall and climbed over. Flames licked at her hands and face. A spark sank into the jacket, and Jennie slapped it out. She needed to get out, but she couldn't leave the horses. *There has to be a way.*

Maybe if she could get the foal out, the mother would follow. Jennie wrapped her arms around the foal. "Come on. Take it easy." She spoke in as calming a voice as she could muster. Jennie managed to escape the prancing mare's hooves as she ducked out of the stall.

Eric hobbled to the barn door and helped Jennie carry the foal well away from the building. Part of the roof collapsed as Jennie started back in.

"Stay back!" Jennie barely heard Eric above the roar of the fire. The mare whinnied. Hooves slammed against the stall, knocking down one side.

"Come on," Jennie urged. "Just stop fighting and come out."

Eric brushed past her and ducked into the building.

"No!" Jennie started after him. A beam shifted and tossed a load of burning shingles at her feet. She jumped back, but not fast enough. A spark shot up to her face, stinging her cheek like a hot poker.

"Whoa. Easy, girl." Eric's plea sounded over the roaring fire.

The mare quieted, but only for a second.

"Come on, Eric. Hurry," Jennie yelled. "Get out of there. Now!"

He didn't respond. The mare's frantic cries stopped.

"Eric!" Jennie backed away from the intense heat. He'd never be able to make it out of there. Jennie dropped down next to the foal and gathered the frightened pony in her arms. She let out a shuddering breath. If he wasn't out by now, he wasn't going to get out at all.

16

Tears stung the burn on Jennie's cheek and dripped onto the foal's silky coat. Snow seeped into her jeans, but she didn't care. She closed her eyes and waited as grief rocked her. She hadn't known Eric long, but she realized now how close a friend he'd come to be.

A horse snorted. She felt its breath on her neck. She sniffed and looked back through watery eyes, expecting to see Faith or Sable.

"Hey," a raspy voice greeted. "You didn't give up on us, did you?" Eric coughed and slid off the mare's back.

Jennie jumped up and threw her arms around his neck. "Oh, Eric. Thank God. I thought for sure you . . ." She buried her face in his jacket.

Eric slid his good arm around her waist and held her close. He smelled of smoke and sweat and blood. Remembering his gunshot wound, Jennie stepped back. "How's the arm?"

He cupped his shoulder. "Must not be too bad. I'm still alive. I think it's bleeding again though."

"Better let me have a look." Eric shrugged off his smoke-blackened jacket while Jennie returned to the truck to get the flashlight. Ordering him to sit down, she examined the wound. It was bleeding, but not badly. The bullet had grazed the surface, leaving a gash about an inch long and a quarter inch deep. Using Eric's pocketknife, she made a slit in the lower part of his T-shirt and tore off about a six-inch band, then secured it around his upper arm and shoulder.

"That was a stupid thing to do." She tied the ends and helped him put his shirt and jacket back on.

"Yeah, well, I couldn't let her burn." He coughed again.

"How did you manage to get her out?"

"Jumped on her back and rode her out. Found a hole on the other side of the barn. Made it through just before it collapsed."

"So what do we do now?" Jennie turned her attention back to the burning buildings. The fire had died down some, looking like a gigantic bonfire. The explosions had stopped now that the fuel had burned down. Both buildings had been reduced to a pile of rubble.

Lights flickered in the distance. Moments later, Jennie heard the sound of approaching horses. She scrambled to her feet, turning off the flashlight. "They're coming back."

In the fire's glow, Jennie could make out the shapes of three horsemen.

"Come on, let's get out of here." Eric took hold of her arm and started running toward the darkness.

"Eric! Jennie!" a deep, familiar voice yelled.

Eric jerked to a stop and waited for the three men to come alongside.

"We saw the fire from the compound." Stan dismounted. "Noticed your horses were gone. When we couldn't find Jennie, we went looking for you. What's going on?"

"Why were you looking for me?" Jennie asked.

"Never mind that now. What happened out here?"

After getting drinks of water from the men's canteens, Eric and Jennie explained.

"You should have come to me, Eric—or to Donovan. With all that's happened around here lately, you had no business coming out here alone."

"I wasn't . . ."

Stan gave Jennie a disapproving look. "You both could have been killed. Did you get a look at the men who did this?"

"No," Eric and Jennie responded together.

He frowned and adjusted the brim of his hat. "And they didn't hang around after you drove the truck out?"

"No. I guess with all the noise from the fire, they didn't hear us. They were already driving away when we got out of the truck."

Stan nodded. "Good thing." Turning to the other two men, he said, "Doesn't look like there's much we can do here. You two can stay and make sure the fire doesn't spread to the house. I'll take the kids back."

"No!" Jennie hadn't meant to protest so loudly. It just came out. "I mean, what about the fire department? And the sheriff? They'll want a statement. Eric and I need to tell them what happened."

"We can handle that," Daniel said. "If the sheriff has any questions, he'll know where to find you."

"But—"

"Eric needs medical attention. Looks like you could use some too." Stan tilted her chin and eyed her face. "You've got a nasty burn on your cheek."

"It's not so bad." Jennie wanted to stay. She needed to talk to the authorities herself. She finally told him so. "I want to know if they found my parents and why they haven't come for me."

"We've been wondering about that too. In fact, Donovan told me this evening that we needed to contact the sheriff again. He must be having trouble finding your family." He nodded toward the fire. "But don't worry. He'll be here. Pretty hard not to miss a fire like that."

"It's obvious that the fire was meant to destroy evidence," Jennie said.

"They took my parents. I'm afraid they might have killed them."

"Let's hope not." Stan frowned. "Don't jump to conclusions, Eric."

"The plane." Jennie suddenly remembered seeing parts of it under the tarp. "They moved all the pieces of the plane into the shop. Why would they do that?"

"Maybe they were instrumental in causing the crash," Stan suggested. "If so, they couldn't chance an FAA investigation."

Causing the crash . . . It had been an accident, hadn't it? Jennie's stomach lurched as she remembered the last few terrifying moments of the crash. What Jennie had thought was lightning—could it have been a bullet?

Jennie rubbed at her temples. "How could they move something so big? There are no roads around the crash site. . . ."

"Helicopters."

"They must have a huge operation."

"They want to get rid of us," Eric said. "And it looks like they'll do anything to make that happen."

"Sadly, Eric, you may be right. Go back to Donovan. Tell him what happened. My men and I will stay here and talk to the authorities."

Jennie's brain felt like mush. She couldn't think. Her throat felt parched from the smoke. She had a headache and hadn't had any juice for hours. Maybe the men were right. She and Eric should go back to the compound. Still, she'd feel better talking to the authorities herself.

"Jennie." Stan settled a hand on her shoulder. "There's something you need to know before you head back—the reason we went looking for you in the first place."

Jennie frowned. "What's that?"

"Your grandmother's condition has worsened."

17

"What's wrong with her?" Urgency rose in Jennie's chest, making it hard to breathe. "Is . . . is she . . ."

"I don't know. Something about her heart. Donovan and the doctor thought you would want to see her."

"When—I mean, how long ago?" She cast Eric an angry look. If he hadn't wanted to come out here, she'd have been there for Gram. What if she already. . . ? Jennie stopped the thought before it fully formed in her mind. Gram was alive. She was tough and healthy. Jennie fought against the images of Gram lying in a hospital bed in a ward without adequate care and equipment. She had to stay positive. And she couldn't blame Eric. She'd encouraged Eric to come back to the farm. She had no one to blame but herself.

"You can stay out here with us if you want to," Stan said, "but—"

"No. You're right. I need to get back." A sickening lump settled itself in the pit of her stomach.

Stan promised to keep them informed as Jennie and Eric mounted the horses and rode off. On a rise two miles away, they could still see the fire's glow. So far there had been no sirens. No headlights from other vehicles. The authorities weren't coming. Jennie wondered if the sheriff didn't know or if he and others in the area were ignoring it. Eric's ranch was a long way from civilization. Still, wouldn't someone have reported it? Apparently even a fire like the one they'd witnessed could go unnoticed out here. Or maybe the authorities had no intention of responding.

It made sense in a warped kind of way. If the ranchers wanted to get rid of the Colony, maybe the sheriff did too. It would explain why Jennie's parents hadn't been notified.

For a brief moment Jennie let herself entertain the thought that her family had been notified and had chosen to leave her there. She knew in her heart that couldn't be true. *They'll come,* she reassured herself. *But until then, you have to take care of Gram and try to figure out what's going on.*

Neither she nor Eric spoke much during the trip back. She was lost in prayers and thoughts about Gram. Eric seemed steeped in grief over losing his parents and his brother. Or maybe wondering, as she was, if they were alive, where they might be.

The long trek back gave her time to think about a lot of things. None of them very pleasant. Questions continued to buzz around her head like a swarm of yellow jackets. Where were her parents? What was taking so long? Where was the sheriff in all this? Was Stan a government agent? He seemed to be keeping an eye on her and Eric. Could the government be investigating the Colony and not want her and Gram picked up?

"Eric, what do you know about the two men who were killed?"

He shrugged. "They were nice guys. Hadn't been with us too long."

"How long?"

"Two or three months." Eric cast her a suspicious glance. "Why?"

"Just curious. Their deaths are probably tied to your parents' disappearance."

"I'm sure they are. I told you, this vigilante group— whoever they are—won't stop until they see every last one of us in the grave."

"Do you know how they were killed?"

"Shot."

"At the same time?"

Eric sighed. "No. The shootings were about a week apart."

"Do you think the sheriff is in on it?"

Eric pondered her question and nodded. "That's possible. He doesn't like the Colony or the people in it."

"Why do you think so? What does he do that makes you suspicious?"

"Humph." Eric rubbed the back of his neck. "I can just tell. He wants us out of there. I think he's afraid there's going to be another incident like there was in Waco, Texas. Remember that weird religious cult? Federal agents wiped them out."

"They brought it on themselves," Jennie said in the government's defense. "They had weapons. Their leader was a sick man."

"Maybe he was, but a lot of innocent people died. Same thing could happen with us. We have no weapons—"

"Stan does," Jennie interrupted. "So do the other men."

"For protection. We're not doing anything wrong, but what if the government came in and tried to force us out? The people here will try to defend themselves. I don't care what anyone says. We aren't some weird religious cult, Jennie. The people at Desert Colony are devoted followers of Christ. We should be able to worship and live as we please. It's one of our freedoms as U.S. citizens."

"The government won't interfere as long as you're living within the law."

"Tell that to the sheriff and his vigilantes."

Eric seemed certain now that the sheriff was involved. Jennie almost wished she hadn't mentioned it. She hated thinking a law enforcement officer might be one of the bad guys. While there were a few, most, like her father, grandfather, and grandmother, were sincere and honest. "I don't know, Eric. I'd hate to think . . ."

"They've got the power to make it look like we're doing something wrong. Want to know why they took my parents away and burned the house down?"

"Apparently to destroy evidence."

"Yeah, but why my family? I'll tell you why. Because I'm one of the Desert Colony people. I think this is a setup, and we're going to get the blame."

Without letting her respond, he went on. "They killed two of our men, and the sheriff accuses Donovan. He's going to accuse us of this too. We are innocent, Jennie, but they'll make us look guilty. If they do, there's nothing to stop them from forcing us out, even if they have to blow the place up to do it."

There was a bitterness in Eric's voice she'd never heard before. Jennie could understand why, but she didn't like it. In fact, his response worried her. He could be right. The people who wanted them out could commit all sorts of crimes and plant evidence to make Donovan and his people look guilty. And if the sheriff had a hand in it, the federal authorities would believe him. They might send undercover agents into the area to find out what was going on.

Jennie had another wild thought. If they'd sent Gram to take photos, could they have had agents in place at the compound? The two men who'd been shot? The men may have learned too much or confided in the wrong people. If only Gram would come around. She'd know. Jennie was sure of it.

"Go ahead," Eric said when they reached the barn. "I'll take care of the horses."

"Thanks." Jennie raced into the compound across the yard and up the hospital steps. The door was locked. She beat on it with both fists, dumping her anger and frustration into the wood.

A woman in a navy dress and white apron finally opened it. Shushing Jennie, she came out and closed the door behind her. "You'll wake the patients. What do you want?"

"I need to see my grandmother."

"It's three in the morning." Though Jennie didn't remember seeing her before, the woman seemed to recognize her. "Oh." Her annoyance slipped behind a forgiving face. "I'm afraid that's not possible right now."

"Why? Stan said she was worse. What's wrong?" Jennie's stomach had wound itself into a tight coil.

"Not worse, really. She became extremely agitated during the night. We had to sedate her."

"He said it was her heart."

"Her heart?" She looked puzzled. "He told you that?" Jennie nodded.

"Well, it wasn't her heart, though her pulse rate has been somewhat erratic. Although," she added thoughtfully, "we did think it might be her heart early on, but it wasn't."

"Why can't I see her?"

"She's resting. She's had a rough night." Looking Jennie over, the nurse said, "You look like you could use some rest yourself. Come in and let me see that burn. We have some special ointment that will heal it quickly and minimize the scarring."

Jennie nodded and followed the nurse into a treatment room.

"By the way, I'm Sheila. What happened?"

Lying down on the exam table, Jennie briefly told her about the fire.

Sheila made clicking sounds to show her disapproval. "I can't believe someone would intentionally start a fire. You poor thing. As soon as I'm finished with you, I'd better check on Eric."

Feeling comfortable with Sheila now, Jennie closed her eyes. It hurt to have the nurse mess with the wound, but the alternative would mean infection. Somewhere between the cleaning of burned skin and dressing it, Jennie dozed off.

It must have been for only a moment or two. When she awoke, she was still lying on the exam table. The nurse had her back turned, and Dr. Paul was standing beside her. The nurse drew something up into a vial. The doctor's gaze drifted from the nurse to Jennie. He smiled when he saw she was awake. "Welcome back. Eric was just telling me about your ordeal."

"Eric's here?"

"Just came in a few minutes ago. Kimberly is dressing his burns."

"How is he?"

"Doing very well. I've got him all sutured up. He should be fine in a few days."

Sheila came toward Jennie, syringe and needle poised.

Jennie sat up so fast, she nearly fell off the table. "What's that?"

Sheila smiled. "An antibiotic."

"Just a precautionary measure, Jennie," Dr. Paul assured. "You don't want that burn getting infected."

Jennie fumbled with the hem of her sweater, lifting it over her head, then raised the sleeve of her turtleneck. She watched the nurse clean a patch of skin, then sink the needle into her arm. Sheila plunged the milky-looking liquid into Jennie's muscle and swiftly pulled the needle out, rubbing the injection site with a cotton ball.

It ached. Jennie slipped her arm back into her sweater. "Dr. Paul, what happened to Gram?"

Sheila looked annoyed. "I told her that Mrs. Bradley had been agitated."

"I just want to know why," Jennie said.

Dr. Paul brought his gaze to meet Jennie's. "We're not certain. I suspect her head injury may have caused some sort of paranoia. She was extremely combative."

"I'd like to see her. I won't wake her up." Jennie slipped off the table, her legs unsteady. "Please."

Sheila and Dr. Paul looked at each other. He gave her a brief nod. "Go ahead, but only for a few minutes."

Jennie left the exam room and tentatively crept down the center of the ward. The overhead lights were still off, leaving only a dim night-light near each of the beds. It was enough. Gram looked peaceful. Surprisingly no worse than she had the day before. If anything, she had more color. Jennie pulled a chair as close to the bed as she could without touching it. She wanted so much to crawl in beside Gram and cuddle up like she had so many times in the past. Instead, she rested her arms and head on a corner of the bed near Gram's feet. Tears welled up in her eyes and slipped silently onto the white bedspread. Gram's foot moved. Jennie jerked up.

Gram lifted her right hand, then let it drop. Her eyes opened. Jennie smiled and scooted forward. "You're awake," she whispered.

Gram put a finger to Jennie's lips and furtively glanced toward the nurses' station, where the doctor and two nurses were talking to Eric. Or rather listening. Eric must have been telling them about their crazy night. Jennie wanted to tell Gram too.

Gram reached up and brushed Jennie's bangs aside. When her fingers brushed the bandage on Jennie's face, she paused.

"It's a long story," Jennie said softly.

Gram closed her eyes.

"What's going on?" Jennie whispered. "They said you were worse."

"Go now." Gram mouthed the words so softly, Jennie could barely hear. "Find Lois. She'll explain."

Jennie didn't understand why, but after promising to be back later in the morning, she kissed Gram good-bye. When she reached Eric and the others, Jennie told them she was going to bed for a while. Eric opted to walk back to the dorms with her.

"How is she?" He took hold of Jennie's hand. The gesture warmed her.

"Okay, I guess." As much as she wanted to tell him what Gram had said, she wouldn't. Not until she'd had a chance to talk to Lois. She and Gram must have talked. "Better in a way."

"Good." Eric seemed preoccupied and sullen. He dropped her off at the dorm and went on to the men's side.

Before going to bed, Jennie showered, taking care to keep her bandage clean, which wasn't an easy task. She was filthy, her skin nearly black from the smoke. Her clothes smelled so bad, she actually considered dumping them in the trash as she peeled them off. Once she'd finished her shower, Jennie slipped into a clean cotton nightgown, bundled her clothes in the towel, and set them just inside the door to her room. She quickly banded her hair in a scrunchie and crawled into bed.

Even though Jennie's mind whirled with unanswered questions—more now than before—she slept. Maybe it was the injection she'd received at the hospital, or maybe it was knowing Gram was getting better, or having someone to talk to who might have some answers. Jennie slept through breakfast and didn't awaken until the noon bell.

She wasn't surprised to find her clothes missing and a clean dress lying across the foot of her bed. Marilee had been busy. Jennie dressed quickly and rushed into the dining room, eager to find Lois. The older woman wasn't there. After filling her plate, Jennie took a seat next to Marilee and Eric.

"Where's Lois?" she asked, trying not to seem too eager.

Marilee looked up from her lentil soup. "You haven't heard?" Her face clouded. "Oh, you wouldn't have."

"Heard what?"

"Lois is in the hospital." Eric kept his gaze on his spoon until it reached his mouth.

"What do you mean, in the hospital? She isn't sick, is she?"

"Not exactly. It happens sometimes—you know, as people get older. I didn't think Lois would get it, but . . ." Marilee set her spoon down and picked up a whole-grain roll. "She has dementia."

Jennie felt like she'd been rammed in the stomach. She'd awakened feeling optimistic. Gram wouldn't have told her to find Lois without a reason. Jennie assumed the older woman knew something—could answer at least some of the questions Jennie had. Now she had no one.

18

The food in Jennie's mouth tasted like ashes. She pushed her plate back and started to take a sip of juice, then stopped. She held it in midair, examining the orange liquid. Marilee eyed her warily. Jennie pretended to take a sip and casually set the glass on the table. "I'm going to see Lois."

"Now?" Marilee and Eric both looked at her as though she were crazy.

"I have to see her and my grandmother."

When she went to get up, Eric put a restraining hand on her arm. "Wait."

"Why?" Jennie glanced around and saw for herself. Her announcement had caught the attention of several residents. One of them was Dory, the older woman who'd told her about the juice being a healthy drink. When Jennie caught her gaze, she looked away. Jennie wished she were better at reading faces. Something in the woman's face sent Jennie's intuition into overdrive. She knew something. Jennie had seen Lois and Dory together and assumed they were friends. She wondered how close they were and if Dory might know what Lois and Gram had talked about. Maybe Lois had confided in her. She'd find out soon enough.

"I want to go too," Eric said, "as soon as we finish eating."

Eric's gaze held a warning. Jennie took it to mean they

shouldn't be drawing attention to themselves. He was right.

Jennie settled back down and began eating, or rather moving food around on her plate. Fortunately, Eric was a fast eater. A few minutes later, he pushed himself away from the table and gathered up his dishes.

"I'd like to come with you," Marilee said, "but I have dish duty. Tell Lois I said hi and I'll come over to see her later."

"I doubt she'll understand." Eric grimaced. "You know how they get. She probably won't even recognize me."

"I know," Marilee said, "but the nurses say we need to talk to them anyway. You never know what they might be hearing."

Eric grumbled something Jennie didn't understand.

"Jennie," Marilee said as they picked up their dishes, "I took the liberty of washing your clothes. They're drying now."

"Thanks. You didn't have to do that."

"Oh yes, I did. I did Eric's too. I just hope the smoke smell comes out. It was horribly strong."

"I appreciate that. And the dress. Thanks."

Marilee smiled. "I like doing things for people. I'll take your clothes back to your room as soon as they're done."

They dropped their dishes off, and as Jennie turned around she nearly ran into Dory.

"Oh, I'm sorry." Dory smiled up at her, looking as though they shared a secret. Did they? Jennie wanted to talk with the woman, but it would have to wait until she could get her alone. Then she would have to be careful. Very careful. Dory could have had something to do with Lois's sudden illness.

Jennie waited until she and Eric were outside before asking, "What did you mean back there—about knowing how *they* get. Do very many of the older residents have dementia?"

"No. Not a lot." He tossed her an aggravated look that said he didn't want to talk about it. "It just happens sometimes."

Fine. Jennie didn't plan to say another word. They walked in silence through the courtyard and into the hospital. Jennie made a point to look at each of the patients as she walked by on her way to Gram's bed. There were only three besides Gram and Lois. Two older men who looked like skeletons with skin. They appeared to be asleep. A woman with stark white hair that stood up at odd angles had the head of her bed elevated. She was still eating, and her hand shook as she brought a piece of bread to her mouth.

Jennie smiled as she walked by. The woman glared at her but didn't speak.

"That's Gladys," Eric said. "She thinks everyone is out to get her."

Maybe they are. Jennie didn't put voice to her thoughts. This wasn't the time or the place. When she approached Gram's bed, Jennie's heart dipped like a plane suddenly losing altitude. Her eyes were glazed over again, staring at some unknown spot across the room.

"Gram." Jennie squeezed her hand. She didn't respond. Her eyelids fluttered shut, seeming to close Jennie out. A deep and sudden sense of loss gripped her. "Gram," she whispered, her tone urgent. "I need you. Please wake up. Please." She waited for several minutes, but Gram gave no indication that she'd heard.

Jennie started to step away, then remembered something Marilee had said. *"You never know what they might be hearing."*

Jennie leaned close to Gram's ear and told her about Lois. "I'm scared, Gram. Really scared. I don't know who I can trust."

"You're a McGrady," Jennie could almost hear her grandmother say. *"Trust your instincts."*

Her instincts. Jennie wished she could. She wasn't even

sure what they were anymore. Jennie had a lot of suspicions but no evidence to back them up. She had too many questions. Too many rabbit trails. Eric's missing family. The fire. Two murders. These had all happened outside the compound. Inside, there were other things going on, like feeling she'd been drugged and Lois's having dementia just when Gram told Jennie to talk to her. That was no coincidence.

Maybe what she needed to do was separate things out, concentrate on what was happening inside the compound and let the outside stuff go. She couldn't deal with it all at once. She'd learned that a long time ago. *"When things get too complicated and overwhelming,"* Gram had often told her, *"take one problem and work on it."*

"Jennie." Eric came up behind her.

She jumped. "Oh, you scared me." She'd completely forgotten about him.

"Sorry. Did you want to see Lois?"

"Um . . . sure. Did you already see her?"

"Yeah. She's okay."

Wanting to see for herself, Jennie followed Eric to the bed at the end of the room. A curtain partially hid the bed. Jennie peeked around it. Lois had the same glazed look about her that Gram had. There was no doubt in her mind now. Lois and Gram had both been drugged. She knew why—at least she thought she did. Most likely Gram had talked to Lois, maybe given her vital information—information she was supposed to share with Jennie. Someone must have found out and wanted her out of the way. Dr. Paul? One of the nurses? Donovan?

"They're being drugged," Jennie told Eric as they left the building. "Can't you see that?"

"They're sick and confused. The doctor has to give them something."

"But he's knocking them out. That isn't necessary. They can't even talk to us."

"Leave it alone, Jennie." Eric walked faster, as though

he wanted to get away from her. He probably did.

"Gram told me to talk to Lois. Then all of a sudden Lois has dementia. Do you think that's a coincidence?"

"Quit making a big deal of it. Lois is an old woman. It happens."

"Not that fast. It takes months, sometimes years, for the symptoms to progress to where they need to be hospitalized. You'd have seen changes. Memory loss."

"You sound like a doctor or something. How would you know?"

"I've seen it. My Grandma Calhoun had Alzheimer's."

"That's not the same thing. I've seen people with that too. With the kind of dementia Lois has, they can be fine one day and the next—boom—they're totally out of it."

"The only thing that would bring it on so fast would be drugs. I don't see how you can be so naïve," Jennie said, exasperated.

"You're saying someone here is purposely knocking out old people?"

"Not just old people. I think everyone is being drugged. Some are getting more than others. Someone here—either Dr. Paul or Donovan . . . maybe both—are putting some kind of tranquilizer into that juice stuff you drink all the time."

"You're wrong. There's no reason—"

"Eric is right, Jennie."

Jennie gave a startled cry. A figure stepped out from behind a building. Donovan.

How much had he heard? Jennie wondered.

He gave her the kind of smile one might give a little kid. "I'm sure it must seem strange to you, but there's an explanation. Lois is indeed being drugged, but not in the way you mean. Our patients often get a sedative to help them relax so that their bodies can heal."

"It turns them into zombies. My grandmother can't even talk to me."

"It helps them to rest."

"What about your juice? Nearly every time I drank it, I got a weird feeling—like I was tired and . . ."

"Peaceful. Yes, there are wonderful things in our juice. Additives to promote health and well-being. There is nothing sinister about it. If you'd like, I'll show you where our juice is made. Perhaps that will ease your mind. Also, we can talk with Paul. His sedatives are only given when a patient needs them."

"I tried to tell her that," Eric said. "She has this idea that we're some kind of evil cult."

"I didn't say that."

"We must be patient with her, Eric. She's not one of us. Jennie doesn't understand our ways or our dedication." Donovan's calm, gentle way of talking seemed to negate her suspicions. His answers seemed almost plausible. She was losing her edge again. She wanted to be angry and upset and found herself calming down instead. And she hadn't had any of the juice. Maybe it wasn't the juice. The food? Or maybe it was Donovan himself. He hadn't touched her or given her anything. Yet when he spoke . . .

She felt confused and unsure of herself around him. His voice carried so much authority. *He knows you're wavering.* Jennie could see the confidence build in his eyes.

"Would you like to see how we make our juice? I'll be happy to take you on a tour myself."

"No. That's okay. I don't need to see it. Maybe tomorrow." It would have been a waste of time, but she didn't tell him that. He'd show her exactly what he wanted her to see. "I believe you," she added. "I'm sorry I doubted you."

"Considering what you have been through, it's understandable. Even one of Christ's own disciples doubted Him."

"Thomas. He had to see to believe. I guess I haven't seen enough yet."

Donovan smiled again. "I should apologize for interrupting your discussion. I wasn't eavesdropping as you may have suspected. I was looking for you, Jennie. The sheriff came by this morning while you were napping. The authorities have been trying to locate your parents, but without an actual address, there isn't much they can do. There are a lot of hotels, and so far he hasn't been able to find them."

"They're not in a hotel, they're in a cabin. It belongs to a friend of Gram and J.B.'s." Jennie's voice rose with irritation. "Why didn't he talk to me?"

"No need. He said he has left numerous messages on the answering machine at your home and at your father's office. I'm sure they'll check in sooner or later."

"What about the fire at Eric's ranch? He should have gotten a statement from me."

"Apparently he didn't feel it was necessary. He talked with Eric."

Jennie tossed Eric an irritated look. "You didn't tell me."

"Didn't have a chance. Anyway, it didn't do much good. He accused me of setting the fire myself, which makes you an accomplice."

"What?"

"Well, not exactly, but he may as well have. Kept grilling me on why we were out there."

"Did you tell him about the men we saw? They shot you. Did you show him the wound?"

"Of course."

"And Gram's plane? Did you tell him about the pieces in the shop?"

Donovan's eyebrows shot up. "Plane? I'm afraid I don't understand. What does the fire have to do with your grandmother's plane?"

"I think that's why it was set—or at least one of the reasons. Someone hauled the pieces to the ranch. They were hidden under a tarp in the machine shop. Whoever did it was destroying evidence."

"I see. No one mentioned this to me . . . Eric?"

"I forgot," Eric huffed. "It didn't seem important. I

was upset. My parents are still missing, and the sheriff is acting like I killed them."

Donovan cupped Eric's good shoulder. "I know. This is difficult for you. You must trust God in all of this, my son. I'm afraid the ordeal is far from over." To Jennie he said, "You shouldn't have gone out there. Your interference has only worked to complicate matters."

"If Eric and I hadn't gone, we wouldn't have been able to rescue their furniture. I—"

"She saved my life." Eric came to her defense.

"Does the sheriff really suspect Eric?" Jennie brought the conversation back.

Donovan nodded. "Not only of the arson, but of killing the two men."

"How could he possibly think that?" Jennie pushed her bangs back.

"Apparently the gun used to shoot them was found near Eric's house."

"That makes sense." Eric rotated his injured shoulder. "Whoever shot them must have used the same gun to shoot at me. Since there's no bullet in the wound, that would be hard to prove. The sheriff thinks I dropped the gun—that I meant for it to burn in the fire."

"He can't seriously believe you were in on this, Eric," Jennie said. Even though she'd considered the sheriff a suspect, she felt duty-bound to defend him—at least until she had proof. "He's just looking at possibilities."

"Eric is right to be worried." Donovan shifted his gaze from Eric to Jennie. "From the start, the sheriff has suspected one or more of our people of killing the men. We couldn't understand his reasoning. They were part of our sect. They were brothers. We had no motive."

"Has that changed?"

"Significantly," Donovan answered. "I just learned that both men were federal agents."

"I was right," Jennie murmured.

"Pardon me?" Donovan frowned.

"Um . . . nothing. I was just wondering why federal agents would come out here. Were they working undercover?"

"Apparently so."

"Do you know why?" Jennie asked.

"I can guess. The locals don't want us here. It's no secret that we produce herbs, and perhaps they, like you, think we have ulterior motives."

"You mean like drugs?"

"Ridiculous, isn't it? Of course, we can't fault the government. I'm certain the locals have been spreading rumors."

"And the agents end up dead." Jennie chewed on her lower lip.

"I'm afraid that whoever did it is framing Eric." Donovan sighed deeply. "You must not despair, brother. We'll all be in prayer about this."

"If the sheriff thinks you're guilty, why didn't he arrest you?"

Eric glanced toward the gate. "I don't know."

"I don't think he has enough evidence," Donovan said.

Jennie rubbed her forehead to ease away the beginnings of another headache. "I'm sorry, Eric. You should have had the sheriff talk to me. I could have cleared it up. I was there when you were shot, remember?"

"I'm being set up. I don't think anything you could say would change his mind. Remember, he thinks you're an accomplice."

Jennie started to tell them she was a cop's daughter, that her grandmother and grandfather had worked as federal agents. She checked herself. Two federal agents had been killed. She didn't want Gram to be next.

19

Come to the kitchen at eleven tonight. The note Jennie had gotten from Dory at dinner gave no other details. She glanced at her watch. Another forty-five minutes to go. After the evening meal, Jennie had gone to her room. Instead of getting ready for bed, she'd changed into her jeans and sweater. Though Marilee had washed them, the faint burn odor lingered. When she got home, she'd throw them away, but she needed them now.

Jennie had tried taking a nap but couldn't sleep. She wanted answers—now. Jennie found a pen and paper in the drawer of the small desk in her room and began mapping out details of what had happened since her unplanned arrival. The plane crash. Finding the cave. Meeting Eric. Coming to the compound. Gram showing up. The two murders. Eric's missing parents and brother. The arson fire. Jennie mulled over in her mind her grandmother's purpose in taking those photos of the compound as they'd flown over. Her first instinct had been drugs. Gram hadn't told her she was wrong.

She went to the closet and took out the bag of Gram's personal effects that Donovan had given her. The men had found them when they went to search for her. Gram's camera was in it.

"Too bad I can't develop the film." Jennie put the camera to her eye and, opening the shutter, started to snap a picture. The lever depressed, but the film didn't advance.

Jennie examined the camera more closely. Someone had taken out the film.

Had Gram done that herself? Jennie dug through the bag for completed rolls of film but found none. Strange. Stan and his two buddies had found the wreckage and taken Gram's bag from it. They would most likely have been the ones to take the film out. But why would they do that? Had they found something else in the wreckage or in her bag that made them suspect she was an agent?

Jennie chilled as the possibility hit her. What if they had found Gram in that wreckage and brought her to the Colony? Jennie shook her head. Why would they lie to her?

What if they did? Jennie's thoughts persisted. Had they also moved the plane to Eric's parents' place? They couldn't have—not with horses, anyway.

Jennie put that part of the puzzle aside. As she'd told Eric, to move the wreckage would have taken a major effort, not something anyone here had the means to do. Unless things were not as simple here as Donovan wanted everyone to believe.

"They have the airstrip," Jennie murmured. And an underground system of tunnels, some of which were off limits to the residents. Still, moving Gram's plane from the crash site didn't make sense unless someone wanted it to look like the plane had never been there.

She rubbed her eyes and flopped onto the bed. Lying there staring at the ceiling, Jennie's brain felt like a computer that had run out of memory and crashed. There were just too many factors.

There was much more to the Desert Colony than a congregation bent on becoming more Christlike. She closed her eyes and took several deep breaths, coaxing herself to relax. Her mind took another course. Jennie thought about Lois and what she'd said about things being different now than when Donovan's father had been alive. The security system, the compound's outer walls . . .

Jennie didn't trust Donovan. Her first impression had

not been a good one. Instincts told her he was not what he seemed. She suspected now that he'd been using some sort of drug to manage his flock, to keep them docile and ignorant. This business about experiencing God's peace was a sham. The only time she'd felt this so-called peace since she'd arrived were those times she'd been under the influence of their miracle juice. No way would she call that God's peace.

God's peace came as a result of being in a relationship with Him, knowing and trusting Him above all things. Donovan talked about trusting God, but Jennie suspected that his real goal was to have the people trust him.

The more Jennie thought about it, the more she suspected him. Donovan had motive for everything that had happened. He'd said the sheriff thought the two agents had been killed by someone inside the compound. Maybe the sheriff was right. But the killer wasn't Eric. Eric was being framed, all right. Not by outsiders, but by the guy he trusted more than his own father. Now all she had to do was prove it.

"God," she whispered, "please help me. I think Donovan has been brainwashing these people. He's involved in something illegal. But I need help. I don't know what to do."

This was all more than she could handle. Jennie needed to go for help. But how? And where would she go? She thought about sneaking out to the barn again and taking a horse. Both times she and Eric had gone out, Donovan's men had shown up—to bring her back. Was it to keep her from getting to someone who could help or to a phone? She had a feeling that sneaking away without being seen wasn't an option.

Maybe you could fly out. The thought shot through Jennie's mind like a rocket. At first she dismissed it. She couldn't fly. True, she'd practiced a couple of takeoffs and landings, but to actually fly a plane . . . She shook her head. Was it possible? Maybe. Her heart racing, Jennie bounced off the bed. She still had another hour before she was due to meet Dory. Time to check out the airstrip. If there was a plane there, maybe she could . . .

"You're crazy," Jennie chided herself. "There's no way."

———————

Jennie couldn't believe she'd done it and that she was standing not more than a few yards from the hangar. She'd walked out of the dorm and out the front gates, then gone around to the back of the compound. Staying in the shadows, she watched a man light up a cigarette and gaze into the darkness beyond the hangar lights.

So apparently not everyone at the Colony opted for a healthy lifestyle.

The man was obviously guarding the place. A rifle leaned against the doorjamb next to him. Eric had said they used guns for protection . . . but an armed guard? What was he protecting out here? The people, or something else?

Another man joined the guard, handing him a cup of something steamy.

"Thought you might like some coffee to warm you up."

"Thanks." He took the cup and brought it to his lips.

"Anything happening?"

"Quiet as a tomb."

"When's the shipment due in?"

The man shrugged. "Anytime now. They're late."

"Figures."

Jennie wrapped her arms around herself and shivered.

They were expecting a shipment, which meant a plane would be landing tonight. Her heart raced just thinking about the possibilities. Maybe she could use the plane's radio to call for help. Maybe the pilot would take her to Portland.

She looked at the two men again and revised her thinking. Something clandestine was going on. They were waiting for a shipment—of what? Food? Supplies? Those weren't the kinds of things people delivered in the middle of the night. Not things you needed guards for either. More than likely they were expecting a shipment of drugs. Which meant she couldn't very well ask the pilot for help. If she was going to use the plane as a means out, she'd have to somehow sneak on board.

Jennie shook her head. "No way," she mumbled.

"No way what?"

Jennie had felt his presence an instant before he spoke. "Who. . . ?" She spun around, almost colliding with the wide expanse of chest. She stepped back.

"A little late for you to be out, isn't it?" Stan eyed her curiously. "Is there something I can help you with?"

"I . . . um, no. I couldn't sleep, so I decided to take a walk. I was curious about the airstrip and . . ." Her voice trailed off.

"Not much to see."

"I guess not."

"You shouldn't be out here at night. Not with our neighbors still taking potshots at us." He settled a firm hand on her shoulder. "Come on. I'll walk you back to the dorm, where it's safe. You can ask Eric to give you a tour of the hangar and airstrip in the morning."

Jennie didn't argue. She fell into step beside the big man. What part was he playing in all of this? *Are you a federal agent?* she wanted to ask but didn't. He probably wouldn't have told her if he was. And not knowing made it impossible for her to confide in him.

"I was hoping maybe there'd be a plane. I could radio Portland. . . ."

"No need. I spoke with the sheriff today. He's on it."

"But—"

"Jennie, it's only been two days. Be patient. These things take time."

"Right." His reassurance did nothing to ease her mind.

At the door to the dorm, she thanked him and went inside.

———

Wonderful smells of home-baked bread reached Jennie's nose long before she got to the kitchen for her rendezvous with Dory. She found the spry older woman bent over a huge mound of bread dough.

"Come in, dear. Have a seat."

Jennie didn't feel like sitting but hitched herself up on a stool near the door.

"Can I get you some tea or juice?"

"No, thanks." Jennie's stomach felt like lead. Had coming to the kitchen been a mistake? Had she misread Dory's intent? Or did the woman really believe the juice was harmless? "Why did you want to see me?"

Dory glanced past Jennie into the dining room. "Lois told me if anything happened to her that I was to make sure you got away from here. It's not safe."

"I can't leave. My grandmother—"

"There is nothing you can do for her now. She'd want you to go."

Jennie stiffened. "Why? What do you mean, there's nothing I can do?"

Dory patted the dough into a ball, transferred it into a large bowl, and covered it. "Things are not as they seem here, Jennie. For some time Lois and I have been concerned that Donovan and his men are using our facilities for their own gain."

"Like what?"

She washed her hands and picked up a towel. "We don't know. Certain parts of the compound are locked and guarded. We think it may be drugs. There is too much money. Too many changes." She looked up at Jennie. "Not that we've seen anything. It's just that most of the planes come at night. We ask ourselves, why at night? Why not in daylight? And why the secrecy? When those two men were murdered, we became even more suspicious. We are led to believe they were killed by outsiders, people who are intolerant."

"But you don't believe that?"

"We've lived here for many years. We've always been on good terms with our neighbors. That has changed, or so we're led to believe. They no longer want us around. I suppose it's possible, but I can't imagine them killing anyone. There has always been a kind of respect. At least, it used to be that way . . . until Donovan took over."

"Did you know that the two men who were killed were government agents?" Jennie asked.

"No, not until Lois talked to your grandmother. She is certain she will be killed, as well, and fears for your safety. You must leave. It's only a matter of time."

"I have to get her out too." Jennie slipped off the stool. "Can you help us?"

"There is nothing I can do. I shouldn't even be talking to you."

"Are you afraid you'll end up in the hospital?"

She glanced up at Jennie, her eyes moist and dark. "Not afraid. We all end up there eventually. Lois went before her time."

"You make it sound like she's dead."

"She soon will be. As will your grandmother."

"We have to help them."

"There's nothing I can do!" Dory insisted.

Jennie wanted to shake the woman. How could she be so compliant? "Then tell me what to do."

"It's too late. Lois and your grandmother have been taken from the infirmary."

Fear turned Jennie's blood cold. "Where are they?"

"I don't know."

"What do you mean, you don't know?" Jennie pressed her hands to her eyes. She had to keep her cool. Getting angry with Dory would get her nowhere. "Please help me. We can't let Donovan get away with this. I need to contact the authorities. There must be a way."

"Perhaps." Dory stared at her floury hands. "Last night Lois told me she was planning to contact the authorities. I'm not sure how, but she planned to go into the tunnels."

"You mean the ones that are locked."

She nodded. "They all used to be open. Sometimes we'd use them in winter. Donovan blocked off the portion under his quarters and the warehouse. You can only get into them through his quarters. There's a hidden panel in the kitchen pantry in Donovan's quarters. The cupboard to the left of the sink. It's locked." She reached inside her blouse and pulled out a cross on a chain, then slipped it over her head. "This will open it. Just insert the base into the keyhole."

"Have you been inside?" Jennie took the cross and examined the intricate carvings. She never would have known it was a key.

"Not for several years."

"Then how do you know this will work?"

"I'm not certain it will. Lois showed it to me this morning before she . . . took ill."

"Before she was drugged."

Dory didn't respond to Jennie's comment. Her hand shook as she hung the towel she'd used on a rack beside the sink. "I took it from Lois's nightstand this morning. I'm not certain how she managed to get it."

Jennie's head was spinning. She wasn't certain she believed Dory—not completely. Much of what Dory said rang true, but some of it, like her conveniently having the key, smelled of a setup. Still, Jennie had no choice. She had to find a way to save Gram and prayed she wasn't too late. She had to know what was in those tunnels and find out exactly what kind of covert operation Donovan was running. Jennie thanked her and slipped the key over her head.

"Wait," Dory said as Jennie turned to leave. "I'll take you the back way so you won't be seen."

Jennie waited while Dory slipped into a coat. Jennie put her own jacket on as Dory took a flashlight from a hook near the door. Instead of going across the courtyard, they went along a path between the exterior wall and a wooden fence. The path and wall bordered the airstrip and went straight to Donovan's back door. It was locked. Dory took a key from her pocket and let Jennie in, then pointed her in the direction of the pantry. "God be with you, Jennie."

"Is Donovan here?" she whispered. "What if he's still up?"

"He won't be. He takes a sleeping potion every night. I put a little extra into his tea tonight."

"And his men?"

"They'll be busy with their duties."

"Thanks." Jennie wasn't sure what she had to be thankful for. Coming here was dangerous, but what other choice did she have? True, she could have taken a horse and gotten out of there, but they'd just come after her. Besides, she wasn't leaving without Gram.

Jennie stood for some time in the dark kitchen. Lights from outside allowed her to see outlines of a table and chairs. Her feet seemed glued to the floor. When she did move, the wood creaked. She stopped and waited, certain someone would come rushing in to stop her. No one came. Jennie crept into the pantry and turned on the flashlight.

The false cupboard had no shelves, only a couple of brooms and dustpans and a pail with a mop standing in it. She slipped the cross into the keyhole and pulled it out as Dory had instructed her on the way over. It clicked and slid to one side, leaving a black yawning hole. Jennie put the chain holding the cross back around her neck and tucked it inside her shirt, then ventured inside. She found herself in a small room lined with concrete.

There was no musty dirt smell in this part of the underground. There were two hallways—one lit, one dark.

Jennie flashed her light into the dark one first. Three doors lined the wide hall. Two to her left and one at the end of the hall. The doors were closed.

Moving cautiously, Jennie entered the lighted room just to her right. It was spacious—about fourteen square feet. "I knew it," she breathed. Just inside the door to her right was a desk topped with a computer and keyboard. A bank of electronic components made the room look like a command center, which it probably was. On the other side was a door that Jennie suspected led outside, probably to the hangar and airstrip.

Jennie set her flashlight on the desk and moved the mouse to exit the screensaver. The desktop revealed an icon for the same Internet server she used. She clicked it on and waited for the program to come up. When it did, she composed an email to her father. She was about to send it when one of the monitors lining the wall lit up. She could hear two men's voices coming closer, and then she heard a click. They were coming in.

Jennie hit the desktop icon to hide her letter and dived under the desk.

20

The door slid open, and Jennie felt the cold air rush in and engulf her. Jennie huddled back against the wall, praying the men wouldn't see her.

"You're late." Stan walked over to the desk. Jennie hoped he wouldn't notice that the screensaver wasn't on. If he was astute he'd see the minimized AOL box at the bottom of the screen. One click and he'd be able to read her letter. She swallowed hard.

"Had trouble with connections at the other end." The man spoke with an accent—Australian, maybe.

"Where's the guy who usually makes the run?"

"Julio? He's making another drop. But not to worry, mate. Got your usual order. Stuff's pure. What more do you need?"

"You look familiar. Have you made the run before?"

"Sorry, mate. This is my first time."

Jennie's breath caught. She knew that voice. At least she thought she did.

"I got some extra cargo for you to take out," Stan said.

"Oh yeah?" The other man had on jeans and a pair of expensive-looking cowboy boots. "And what might that be?"

"Barrels. Filled with some cargo we need to get rid of. Want you to dump it in the ocean on your way back to Colombia."

"And what is it you might be wanting to get rid of?"

141

"No need for you to know. Better that way. You'll be paid well for your trouble." Stan reached down beside the desk and pulled out a black briefcase. "Ten thousand extra in there for you."

"And all you want me to do is dump these . . . *barrels*?"

"That's it."

Jennie leaned forward to get a better view. Stan stood with his back to her now. His bulk nearly obliterated her view, but she'd seen all she needed to. The pilot had nearly white hair. Being of English and Irish descent, he could easily speak with an Aussie accent. Jennie had never been so happy to see anyone in her life. She had to cup her hand over her mouth to keep from cheering. She should have known J.B. would come through. He loved Gram and had to have known what she was doing. He'd come to rescue them. She didn't know how he'd managed it, but he had.

"I don't like it," J.B. said. "That's a lot of money just to dump barrels. If I'm taking on a dangerous job, I want to know the details."

Stan grunted. "Can't say as I blame you. We need to dispose of some bodies."

Jennie's insides crumbled. *Bodies.* He was talking about Gram and Lois. And she had actually considered Stan one of the good guys. How could she have been so wrong?

"How many?" J.B. asked.

"Six."

Jennie gasped. *Six?* It took a moment for her brain to adjust to the shock. Of course—Gram and Lois, and Eric's family. If Donovan was responsible for the death of the two agents, it made sense that he'd be in on getting rid of Eric's family. It would give him more land. More privacy. More space in which to carry out his drug-smuggling operation.

But who is the sixth?

You. The answer came all too clear. Someone was probably looking for her now. Jennie tried to process the information.

"Ah. Six bodies. You've been busy." J.B. had been an agent all his life, but Jennie still couldn't understand how he could stay so calm and appear so callous. He was the kindest, most generous man she knew. She supposed he had to stay in character to stay alive.

"What can I say? It's a nasty business."

"That it is. All right, then. Let's load them up, and I'll be out of here."

Jennie had to find a way to let him know she was there. She had to get aboard that plane.

A beep sounded. Stan pulled a cell phone from his jacket pocket and barked into it. "Yeah." After a moment's silence, he said, "You've got to be kidding." Then, "I'll deal with it."

He placed the cell phone on the desk and took a step toward J.B. "That was Julio's boss. Seems Julio was found in the warehouse. Unconscious."

Stan pulled out a gun. Jennie bit her lip to suppress a cry.

"Really. I wonder what happened." J.B. continued to play his part.

"We'll find out for sure when Ramirez gets here."

"So they're sending a replacement? And here I thought I was doing a pretty fair job."

"Funny man. Somehow I don't think you'll be laughing for long."

"I'm not laughing now."

"Hey, I just remembered where I've seen you," Stan announced.

"And where might that be, mate?"

"There's a picture of you in your wife's billfold, Mr. Bradley."

"So you do have her."

"We do, and we know she's an agent."

"I see. And my granddaughter?"

"That would be Jennie," Stan snorted. "Yeah, she's here. Kid's nothing but trouble."

143

"I take it she and my wife are among the bodies you wanted me to dispose of?"

Stan still had his back to her. So close that if Jennie could work up enough courage, she could tear out from under the desk and tackle him. She held her breath and began to move out.

Stan stepped away, putting himself out of Jennie's reach. "Let's go."

Jennie crouched low and thought about rushing him, but it was too dangerous. He'd see her and probably shoot before she could straighten up. Why didn't J.B. go for his gun? He must have one.

"Where are we going?" J.B. asked.

"For a little walk."

"And if I don't agree?"

"Then you'll get to see me personally put a bullet through your wife's head."

"Can't have that, now, can we? She's still alive, then, is she?"

"For the moment. Behave yourself, and you can spend your last couple of hours together. It's not a honeymoon suite, but . . . what can I say. This place isn't exactly the Ritz."

"I'll take what I can get. Lead on."

"Your gun." Stan extended his hand. "I take it you carry a piece?"

"Be rather foolish of me not to." Stan took J.B.'s gun and set it on the corner of the desk, then pushed J.B. forward toward the door Jennie had come through only minutes before.

Jennie set aside her thoughts of tackling the man—at least for now. He was taking J.B. to Gram. Gram was still alive. Jennie eased out of her hiding place and peered around the corner. At the end of the hall, Stan pushed a button on the wall, and the door slid open.

"Here's another one for you," Stan said to a man who

stood in the doorway with a rifle. "Watch him." He pushed J.B. inside.

"Good grief," J.B. sounded angry now. His pretense was gone. "What have you done to these people?"

Stan didn't answer.

"What's going on?" the guard asked. "I thought we were getting rid of these guys, not bringing in more."

"Long story." Stan explained what had happened. To J.B. he said, "My friend here will take good care of you." Stan hit the button again. As the door slid shut, he turned and came back down the hall toward the office.

Jennie jerked back and took cover under the desk again, grabbing Stan's cell phone and J.B.'s gun on the way down. Stan walked into the office and out through the outer door he and J.B. had entered through earlier. She could hear him telling someone else about J.B.

"Let's get this stuff unloaded," Stan ordered.

"You sure it's the real thing? If the guy was a phony, maybe . . ."

"It's okay," Stan said. "I checked it when he came in."

"All this government activity is making me nervous." Another man came up to the door and walked in with Stan. Jennie hadn't seen him before, but his uniform and badge told her in no uncertain terms who he was. This was the county sheriff. "I think we ought to move the operation."

"Been thinking the same thing. I'll tell Ramirez this will be the last run. We'll drop out for a while and open up somewhere else."

"Do you think the agent was working with anyone?"

"Probably. We'd better hide the plane just in case. I told Daniel to put it in the hangar and douse the lights."

Jennie sat there too stunned to move or think. She had to do something, but what? The plane was sitting on the airstrip waiting for a pilot. She was a pilot—almost. But she couldn't leave the others behind. And at the moment she was trapped under a desk.

If only she could get Gram and J.B. and the others into the plane. Another pilot was coming in. Stan had talked to J.B. about taking the bodies out in barrels. Would they still do that? If Jennie waited long enough, Stan's men would load the plane for her. She'd sneak on board, and when everyone was loaded, she'd get into the cockpit and fly out.

It's a crazy idea, she chided herself. *It'll never work. You've only had three lessons.* Jennie heaved a sigh. Maybe it was crazy, but she was running out of options. And three lessons were better than none.

"Should we load him on the plane with the others?" Stan asked.

"No. I have a better plan. How are you fixed for explosives?" the sheriff asked.

"We have an arsenal . . . why?"

"We're going to blow this place to kingdom come."

"Isn't that taking things too far?"

"Not at all. It'll be tragic, but most cults go down eventually. The Desert Colony will go out in a blaze of suicidal glory, and it'll take the government years to figure out what happened, if they ever do."

"So we make it look like Donovan killed himself and his followers in a mass suicide?"

"That's about it."

"Why not just increase the Ecstasy in their juice?"

Ecstasy? Jennie recognized the name of the popular street drug. So that's what they were putting in the juice. Supposedly it made people feel good. Like most drugs, it was dangerous. And in some cases, deadly.

"That'll take too long. Bombing will be quicker. We just need to make certain no one gets out."

"We'll lock the gates and cover all the entrances. A couple of rifle shots will send them all to their rooms."

Jennie wrapped her arms around her knees. She wished she hadn't come. She couldn't bear to hear about their evil plans—plans she might not be able to do anything about.

146

Thankfully, they walked out again and closed the door behind them.

Jennie eased out of her hiding place. This was a nightmare. It had to be. Soon she'd wake up and be in her bed at home. She choked back her anguish and faced the computer screen. Jennie added what she'd learned to her letter and sent it. Even as she did, she knew there was little or no chance of it reaching her father in time.

She hurried from the office and into the hallway. There she hesitated. Should she try to get J.B. and Gram out now? Face an armed guard? Alone?

She needed help, and the only person she could trust was Eric. Jennie let herself out and stepped back into the pantry in Donovan's kitchen. She thought about waking him and telling him what his men had planned. But would Donovan believe her? She doubted it. He'd probably bring Stan in, and Stan would deny it all. She'd be put under guard with the others. Eric was the only one she dared confide in. Hopefully, when she told him what had happened, he'd believe her. If he didn't, come morning they'd all be dead.

21

Not wanting to wake the others, Jennie went around to the back of the building and knocked on what she hoped was Eric's window. He'd told her the room number. Jennie lined it up with the rooms in the women's dorm and hoped they matched.

He didn't respond. Jennie picked up a rock and tapped on it again. A little too hard. It broke. The falling glass did the trick. Eric rolled over and snapped on his bedside lamp.

"What. . . ? Who is it?" He came to investigate.

"It's me," Jennie whispered. "Be careful of the glass."

Eric yawned and ran a hand through his mussed hair, then eyed the glass-littered floor. "What's going on?"

"Get dressed and meet me outside."

"Now? It's after midnight."

"Just get dressed. I think I know where your family is."

Eric didn't need to hear more. In less than three minute's time he met her at the back of the dorm. They headed toward Donovan's, and Eric listened intently as Jennie told him what had happened.

"I don't know how you expect me to believe you. That's the craziest story I've ever heard."

"I know. I can hardly believe it myself. Come on. I'll show you the computer room, and maybe, if you're still skeptical, we can get into the warehouse where they're storing the drugs."

"I don't care about the drugs. I want to see my family. You're sure they're here?"

"Stan didn't actually say he had them."

"Then what makes you think they're here?"

"Stan said he needed to dispose of six bodies—make that seven with J.B. Gram and Lois make two. Your mom, dad, and brother make five, and I'm probably the sixth. The thing is, I don't know if they're still alive."

He stiffened and took Jennie's hand. "We have to find out."

"There's a guard." Jennie tucked stray hairs behind her ear. "With a gun."

"There's two of us and one of him."

"I only saw one, but there might be others." She pulled him to a stop at Donovan's kitchen door. "I have a plan." She outlined her idea, then added, "If it doesn't work, one or both of us could be killed."

Eric placed his hands on her shoulders. "If what you said is true, we don't have much choice."

Jennie nodded.

He leaned forward and kissed her on the forehead. She put her arms around his waist and rested her head on his chest. For that one brief moment she had an inkling that they could actually pull it off. They were a team. Jennie took a deep breath and let it out slowly. Pulling away, she pushed open the kitchen door, which she'd left unlocked when she went to get Eric. Entering the pantry, Jennie pulled the key and chain from her neck. "Hold this." She handed him the flashlight and inserted the key. The door slid open. Seeing no one, Jennie stepped inside. She crept to the open door of the computer room. "There's no one here." Jennie fingered the gun in her pocket, took it out, and handed it to him. "You might need this."

He winced as he took it and slipped it into his pocket. "I hope not."

"It's the room at the end of the hall. You know what to do."

Jennie led the way, and when they reached the end, he pushed the button, and the door slid open.

Eric pushed Jennie inside.

Jennie stumbled forward, catching herself with her hands as she fell. "Watch it." She twisted around and stood, backing against the wall.

"Hey, Eric. What are you doing here?" The guard scrambled to his feet.

He knows Eric? The hairs on the back of Jennie's neck stood on end. *Why does he know Eric?* Jennie hadn't seen him in the common room or dining area. She hadn't seen anyone wearing fatigues. Of course, he probably only wore them while he was on duty out here.

"Got another one for you."

Eric was good. He didn't even flinch when he saw his parents and brother lying on a pile of handmade quilts. Jennie did. Gram, J.B., Lois, and the others were laid out like corpses. Jennie would have thought them dead if not for the rise and fall of their chests.

"Who is she?" The guard scowled and looked from Jennie to Eric, his gun wavering between the two.

Eric continued to hold the gun on Jennie. "She's the Bradley woman's granddaughter. Boss wants to leave her here with the others. She's been a pain. Keeps trying to escape."

The young man shook his head. "He keeps sending more in. When's he planning on putting them in the plane?"

"You got a point there, James. Plane's empty. It's just sitting out there in the hangar. What do you say we load them in? I'll give you a hand, then you can take a break while I watch them."

He frowned uncertainly. "I don't know."

"Come on. You know it has to be done. Why not get it over with now?"

That wasn't part of the plan. Jennie's gaze fastened on Eric's. He looked away. *He knows the guard. He's one of*

151

them. The thought left as quickly as it came. *He can't be,* she decided. *He knows about the change in plans. He's just trying to get us on board the plane.*

"All right. Let's do it. I could use a break. Haven't seen Marilee in two days. Maybe I'll wake her up and see if she wants to hang out for a while."

"Good plan. She was asking about you this morning."

Marilee? The suspicions came back full force. This guard was Marilee's fiancé, James? Did Marilee know what he was up to? How many of these so-called pacifists were involved in the drug smuggling operation? Could Marilee herself be one of them? And Eric? She'd trusted him. Jennie's mind whirled with possibilities. She had told him everything.

No way. She chided herself again. Eric was on her side. Their goal had been to get on that airplane. He was doing that and getting rid of the guard at the same time.

"Better give her something to knock her out." James opened what looked like a first-aid kit.

"What's that?" Eric asked.

"Not sure. Got it from the infirmary. Knocks them out cold."

"How come you have so much of it?"

"Have to inject these guys every three or four hours." He plunged the needle into the top of the bottle and began to draw out the clear liquid. "Getting tired of it, if you want to know the truth."

"Seems like it would take too long. Why don't we just tie her up?"

"She might make too much noise. This stuff keeps them from talking—kind of paralyzes them. It works pretty fast."

Eric raised his eyebrows as if impressed. "Let me give it to her."

"You know how?"

"Sure. Used to give animals shots all the time on the farm."

Jennie pressed herself against the wall. "Don't. Eric, please."

"Hold the gun on her." Eric turned to Jennie. "I wouldn't fight too much if I were you. This is a lot better than being dead."

Eric pressed her against the wall.

"What are you doing?" She tried to push him away, but he was too strong.

He jerked the jacket off her shoulder and pushed up her sleeve. He then pulled the cap off the needle with his teeth. "This isn't going to hurt a bit."

Jennie squeezed her eyes shut. She knew he wouldn't actually stick the needle in. He'd only pretend to.

"Eric, no!" Jennie cried out as the needle sank into her upper arm.

22

"Ow." *Eric, why? I trusted you.* Jennie's startled gaze latched onto him. He looked away and eased the jacket over her shoulder.

She sank to the floor. Jennie couldn't bear to look at him—to let him see how shocked and dejected she felt. A tear slipped from between closed lids. She brushed it away.

"Let's take the girl first," she heard Eric say. "If this stuff works as fast as you say, she should be out of it by the time we get her to the plane."

"Sure. Let's wrap them up in these quilts. It'll be easier to carry them."

James grabbed a quilt from the corner. He took one arm and Eric the other. She resisted, but her heart wasn't in it. They rolled her in the quilt, and with one at her head and the other at her feet, they carried her out of the room and down the hall.

For several long and painful minutes Jennie believed Eric had actually betrayed her. As she lay in a heap in the cargo hold of the plane, though, Jennie realized that instead of putting the drug into her tissues, he'd shot it onto her sleeve and only pricked her with the needle to make it look real. She felt the wet cloth against her skin. She was still very much alert, and suddenly very hopeful.

She stiffened when she heard them come in again with another load. Not that she could have moved. Her arms were pinned to her sides mummy-fashion inside the quilt.

In just fifteen minutes they had loaded everyone on. Eric slapped James on the back. "I don't know about you, but that was hard work. Those last three guys were heavy. I think we both deserve a break."

"No way. Can't leave them alone. Don't know how long it'll be till the other pilot comes in, and we have to keep them sedated."

"Right. Don't worry about it. I'll stay."

"Great. I'm out of here."

She heard a click, then footsteps. "Jennie, he's gone." He unwrapped the quilt and helped her up. "You okay?"

"Yeah. You had me worried there for a minute. I thought you were one of them."

"Sorry about that. I had to make it look real. He was right there watching."

"I know." She rubbed the injection site. "I don't know how you kept your cool like that."

"Hey, my heart is still going ninety miles an hour. I was scared spitless."

"Me too, but we did it." She wrapped her arms around his neck and hugged him. "All we have to do now is get this thing out of here."

"Help me unwrap everyone first. We don't want them to suffocate."

They removed the quilts. Though they stirred, all of them, including J.B., were still out of it.

"Oh no." Jennie heard the drone of an airplane and a bright light approaching the end of the runway. "It's the new pilot."

Jennie moved up to the cockpit and peered between the seats. The plane was already landing. "I don't think there's enough room for us to get around it."

"Stan," someone yelled, "the prisoners have escaped!"

"Simmer down." Stan's deep voice sounded dangerously close. "We'll find them."

"We're sunk," Eric muttered.

"No. This is the last place they'll think to look for us.

At least until they find James."

"Yeah, well, when they find out he's missing, they'll go straight to Marilee."

"Maybe he and Marilee are out in the hills somewhere. . . ."

Eric rubbed a hand across his mouth. "I doubt it. They're probably in the dining room in plain view."

"Which reminds me. Why haven't I seen him?"

"He's been working a night shift lately. Sleeps during the day."

That made sense. Jennie sucked in a breath and climbed into the pilot's seat. "Everyone's gone inside. If we're going to go, it has to be now."

"I thought you said there wasn't room."

"I'll make room. I just hope I can remember how to fly." *Please, God, get us out of here.* She reached for the ignition.

"The keys . . ." Jennie hit her face and tore her hands through her hair. "I didn't even think about the keys." Panic rose inside her and crashed. Her breath came in gasps. *Stop it! Just calm down.*

"This was a crazy idea. I knew it wouldn't work."

"Be quiet. Let me think." Jennie gripped the controls, willing herself to slow her breathing. *Keys, where are you?* She closed her eyes and imagined J.B. coming in. *Of course.*

"Okay, J.B. flew in. They must be in his pocket."

"I'll check." Eric hurried back to where J.B. lay crumpled on the quilt. After digging into J.B.'s jacket and pant pockets, he came up with the keys. He smiled triumphantly and tossed them to Jennie.

Jennie went through two of them before finding a fit. The other plane had come to a stop about fifty feet from the hangar. Before twisting the key to start the engine, Jennie mentally went through the motions of pushing in the throttle. *Not too hard. Give it enough gas, but not too much.* She imagined herself rolling out of the hangar, around the other plane, going faster and faster, then lifting off.

"Jennie, let's go. What are you doing?"

"Practicing."

He climbed into the seat beside her. "You have flown before, right?"

"Yeah, but only three lessons."

"That's three more than I've had. You can do it. I know you can."

She swallowed back the bile rising to her throat. "I have to."

Jennie twisted the key. The engine started. The propeller started spinning. Jennie eased the throttle, feeding fuel to the engine. She held her breath as the plane began moving.

"Hey!" someone shouted. "What . . . who's in the plane?!"

"Someone stop them! Give me that rifle."

Jennie could barely hear the shouts above the sound of the engine. She didn't know who was talking and wasn't about to look back. She focused on the runway and skirted around the other plane just as the pilot and his passenger were disembarking.

Crunch.

"You hit it." Eric leaned forward. "Wing looks okay. Keep going!"

"I am." Jennie's mouth felt dry as cotton. "Hang on." She shoved the throttle all the way in. A gun shot split the air, then another.

"They're shooting at us." Eric looked back out the passenger window. "There must be half a dozen guys out there."

Jennie leaned back as the end of the runway approached and pulled the yoke back as far as she could, willing the plane to rise.

"You did it!" Eric grinned. "You got us up."

Jennie looked down and back. They were out of shooting range now. All she had to do was fly. Later she would figure out how to land. For now they were safe.

"Eric, I don't believe this. Look!" Glancing down, she saw what looked like an army command post. Four tanks crawled over the desert heading toward the compound. There must have been a hundred men on foot wearing camouflage uniforms and carrying guns.

"Looks like they mean business. Good thing we got out when we did."

"J.B. must have known they were there. Maybe he was supposed to give them a report. When he didn't come back . . ."

"They decided to move in."

"Something like that."

Eric groaned. "Don't look now, but I don't think they want us up here."

A helicopter came up beside them, close enough for Jennie to see his face. The pilot spoke into his radio.

The radio inside the cockpit crackled. "This is the DEA. Turn the plane around and land."

"No . . . we can't."

"I repeat. Turn the plane around and land. I have orders to shoot."

"No!" She shook her head. "Listen to me."

"Better do as he says."

The chopper rose and got above her.

"He's going to force us down!"

"Please, listen. I'm Jennie McGrady. You have to let us go."

Jennie screamed as the feet of the helicopter tapped the top of the plane. "All right. I'm going. But my dad will hear about this!"

Jennie turned the plane around and headed back to the runway. She set up for a straight-in landing, eased back the throttle, and hoped she could keep the plane level.

"I knew it wouldn't work." Eric slumped in his seat.

"Just shut up. They can't just let us fly out. They don't know me. For all they know, I might be transporting drugs. If only Dad were here."

"Well, that's just great." He pointed at the gunman near the hangar. "We've got them coming at us from both sides now. Either way, we're dead."

"What happened to your faith, Eric? We're not finished yet."

Eric stared intently out the window on his side. "Cowards."

"What?"

"Never mind." He covered his head. "You're coming in too fast!"

The wheels hit the ground with a thud. "Eric!" Jennie screamed. "Help me with the brakes. Stomp them hard— with even pressure or we'll roll." They skidded to a stop. The plane's momentum pitched them forward, ramming the nose into the tarmac.

Jennie's seat belt grabbed her and held her in place.

"I thought you knew how to fly," Eric gasped.

"Jennie! Is that you?" a familiar voice came over the radio.

"Dad! Yes, it's me."

"What's going on, princess?"

"It's a long story."

"I don't know what you're doing in that plane, but do not leave. Take cover."

"I have J.B. and Gram and some other people in the plane. I was trying to get away."

"I'm aware of that now. The pilot was under strict orders not to let anyone leave."

"We can't stay here, Dad. They're going to blow the place up."

"Who?"

"The drug dealers. The sheriff is one of them."

"We have a ground troop coming in right now."

"No, Dad, you have to call them off. Stan and his men set charges. I don't know when they're set to go off. Your men will be killed."

"Jennie"—Eric took hold of her arm—"I have a feeling it's going to be soon. While you were busy landing, I saw Stan and his men heading for the stables."

"They're getting away, Dad. We have to go."

"Jennie!" He had a warning in his voice that made her hesitate, but only for a second.

"You have your cell phone?" Jennie asked.

"Yes, but—"

"I'll call you. The men in charge of this whole thing are heading for the stables on the other side of the compound from where you are."

"Your dad's right, Jennie," Eric said. "You stay here. I'll go after them myself. I have a score to settle."

"Eric, wait!"

"We'll take care of them. Can you fly out?" Jennie's dad asked.

"No." She started to open the door and realized her side of the plane was facing the warehouse and the guns. "I'm going, Dad. We have to stop Stan and the others before they get too far away. Once they get out of range, they'll set off the charges."

"We're coming in, Jennie. Just stay put." Dad's words filled the empty cockpit as Jennie slid out of the plane on Eric's side and tore out into the darkness after him.

23

"Jennie, where are you?" Dad sounded furious with her, but she'd had no choice.

She put the cell phone close to her mouth so she could speak softly. "In the stables. But there's no sign of them."

"This is nuts. Get out of there."

"Trust me, Dad, this is much safer than on the airstrip."

"I don't see them." Eric came back to her after checking the stalls.

"Hold on, Dad." She turned to Eric. "Are you sure you saw them come out here?"

"Where else would they have gone? The horses are still here."

Jennie heard a grinding. "What's that?" She ran outside. "I don't believe it. . . . Eric!" Jennie called to him, but he was already standing beside her, mouth open. Half the mountain seemed to open. "Looks like something out of a James Bond movie."

"What's going on, Jennie?" Dad barked.

"We found them. They're going inside the mountain."

"What?"

"It looks like they've built this huge command center inside the mountain. There's a helicopter inside and a bunch of electronic equipment. Stan and another guy are getting into the helicopter."

"Hurry. The doors are closing." Eric took off.

Jennie raced after him, but they were seconds too late. Just as the huge double doors slid shut, Jennie heard the chopper start. "Dad, they're getting away." The chopper wings beat out a staccato pattern and rose up out of the top of the mountain.

"We'll take it from here." Within seconds the government had its chopper over the scene. It forced the helicopter down.

Jennie turned to go when the side door opened again. Donovan jogged out and stopped when he saw them. "Stan's getting away," he panted. "He betrayed us. He's been using us. . . ."

"You're saying you didn't know about it?" Eric asked.

"Of course not. I'd never allow anything like that, and he knew it."

Maybe he was innocent, Jennie considered. "Why are you out here? You were running away with Stan."

"The sheriff—I was trying to talk to the sheriff, but he hit me. He's one of them. I didn't know about the drugs, I swear."

"You're lying." Eric advanced on him.

"It's true," Donovan gasped and began running. At first Jennie thought he was heading back inside the compound, but instead he ducked into the stable. A horse whinnied, and he came racing back out on one of the geldings.

Eric ran into the barn and returned moments later on Sable's back.

Jennie tore out soon after on Faith.

"Jennie, are you still there?"

"Can't talk now, Dad. Donovan is getting away on horseback."

"Which direction?"

"I don't know." She glanced back. Agents were storming the fortress inside the mountain. She could barely see the forms of Eric and Donovan racing over the desert. Jennie told her dad where they were heading and stuffed the cell phone into her pocket. Leaning forward, she urged her mount to race toward the two men. The DEA helicopter rose again and appeared to be searching for them. Its light hit Donovan and Eric and kept them in its beam.

Donovan's horse was fast, but Sable overtook him. Eric came alongside and grabbed Donovan around the waist. Both men toppled onto the ground. It took Jennie only seconds to catch up with them. Donovan lay on his back, whimpering. Eric straddled him, fist in the air, ready to strike. "You knew. You took my parents and were going to kill them."

"No . . . Eric. I didn't. I swear."

Jennie dismounted. "It's over, Donovan."

He whimpered like a whipped pup.

"I'm going to kill the creep with my bare hands." Eric jammed a fist into his face.

"Eric, no."

Eric pulled out J.B.'s gun.

"No, please, don't kill me," Donovan pleaded.

"Why should I listen to you? It was all a farce. Nothing here was real. I believed you." Eric was crying now, tears spilling freely. "I thought I was getting into something real and spiritual. But it was all a hoax."

"Not all of it." Jennie put a hand on his shoulder. "God is real. So is His love. So is faith and prayer."

Eric sat hunched over Donovan, who still lay on the cold ground.

"Please." Donovan whined. "I didn't hurt anyone. I never did. Stan killed the agents. He wanted to kill them all. I tried to stop him, but he wouldn't listen."

"You expect us to believe you?"

"I'm innocent."

"You're pathetic." Eric got to his feet and handed Jennie the gun. "You watch him. I can't stand to look at him." Shoulders sagging, he walked a short distance to the horses and gathered up the reins.

Jason McGrady arrived with several uniformed men,

who took over. Jennie handed over the gun. "It's J.B.'s. I took it when he was captured. Figured it might come in handy." She watched an agent lead Donovan away, and then, glancing toward the compound, she added, "The charges. Stan and the sheriff were going to blow the place up."

"They didn't get a chance," one of the men said. "Thanks to you we have the detonator, and our people are defusing the explosive devices as we speak."

"The residents are being evacuated just in case." Dad's voice came from behind her.

Jennie sighed and leaned against him as his arm curled around her shoulders. "Am I in trouble? I know you said I should wait in the plane, but I couldn't."

He shook his head. "I'd have done the same thing, princess. I'm just grateful you're safe. Come on, let's go. You have a lot of explaining to do."

24

"I'm glad you came with us." Jennie picked up a handful of powdery snow and tossed it at Eric. They'd been cross-country skiing for about an hour. The sun made diamonds on the snow. In the distance Mount Bachelor stood proud and haughty. Tomorrow they'd be on it, flying down the ski slopes and taking hot cocoa breaks in the lodge.

"I appreciate the invitation." Eric tossed a little snow back but kept skiing.

J.B. and Gram had extended their time at the mountain resort for another week. After the ordeal they'd been through, they needed it. Gram and the others had been taken to a real hospital and treated. The drugs they'd been given wore off with no side effects. By the following day they were all discharged. Eric's parents and brother had gone home. With help from friends and neighbors, their things had been moved back into the house. Rebuilding of the barn and shop had already begun.

Things were almost back to normal again. The criminals had been caught and would be facing charges of drug trafficking. The compound had been a perfect drop-off and pickup point, especially with Donovan controlling his followers with small doses of his special blend of peace drugs every day.

"Things are kind of unsettled with my folks," Eric said. "They're glad to have me home again, but I'm not sure I want to be there. And I think they blame me for the fire."

"That's not fair. . . . If you hadn't been there, they would have lost more than they did. And you didn't have anything to do with it."

"I didn't start it. But if I hadn't joined the Colony, none if it would have happened."

"You can't know that. Your brother and father found Stan and his men while they were moving the plane wreckage. You had nothing to do with that. If you hadn't been a member of the Colony, the drug operation would still have been going on. I'm glad you joined. I think God had you just at the right place at the right time. Gram and I needed you to be there."

Eric grinned, and Jennie's heart melted. "I needed you too," he said.

Embarrassed by the admiration in his eyes, Jennie straightened and turned around in the direction they'd come. "We'd better get back."

"Speaking of going back, I wonder . . ." Eric paused.

"What?"

He pressed his lips together. "I've been thinking about going back to Desert Colony for a while. At least until school starts next fall."

"I thought they were closing the place down."

"Lois and Dory and some of the others want to keep it going. There's a lot of work to do—like tearing down the outside walls Donovan built. They want to get it back to the way it was before he came in."

"Do you think they can?"

"With help. My dad and brother are going to volunteer. So are some of the neighbors. At first I didn't want anything to do with them. But now I see that most of the people there are dedicated Christians. The community had a good reputation once, and it can again."

"They're getting rid of the juice, aren't they?" Jennie wrinkled her nose.

Eric laughed. "There was nothing wrong with the original juice. You know that. Donovan managed to doctor every batch."

"Speaking of doctors, what happened to Paul and the nurses? They must have known about Donovan's secret ingredient."

"Actually, they didn't. Donovan was coming in to pray for the patients several times a day. Only, his prayers included a tranquilizer."

"It's hard to believe Paul didn't know. He's a doctor."

"Maybe he was like me and the others. We knew something wasn't right but didn't want to believe it."

"How's Marilee doing? Did she know about James being involved in the drug smuggling?"

"No. James and about a dozen other young guys got recruited to work in the warehouse. Stan gave them a cut of the take, which in some cases turned out to be a lot of money. I imagine if I'd been there longer, they'd have tried to recruit me too."

"Poor Marilee."

"I wouldn't worry too much about her. Knowing Marilee, she's already forgiven him and is ready to move on."

"Is she one of the reasons you want to go back?"

"No, why?"

"I think she likes you."

He leaned back and gave her a wary look. "You trying to set us up?"

"No. I just wondered."

"Marilee isn't my type, so you don't have to worry."

"I'm not worried."

"You looked worried to me."

She gave him a playful jab in the stomach and took off. She raced him to the cabin and won.

Gram and J.B. were deep in conversation when they went inside. "What I don't understand is why it took you so long to find us." Gram was lying on the couch in front of the fireplace, using J.B.'s lap for a pillow.

Jennie and Eric came in quietly and sat on the floor in

front of a chair, her back leaning against Eric's legs. Gram had dozed a lot over the last few days and still hadn't figured out everything that had happened. Jennie was having some trouble with it herself.

J.B. smoothed Gram's short gray hair back from her forehead. "The odds were against us finding you at all, luv. When you didn't show up, we called the airport and learned that you had changed your flight plan and were headed for Sun Valley."

"Sun Valley!" Gram glanced at her husband. "And you believed it?"

"Now, Helen, you have been known to change your plans rather abruptly." J.B. winked at Jennie. "It didn't help that the sheriff had a part in the drug operation."

"Which meant he hadn't tried to find you at all." Jennie wrapped a long tendril of hair around her finger. That was the part of the whole deal Jennie found hardest to swallow. The sheriff and Stan were the major performers in the drug-smuggling business. They, not Donovan, controlled everything. Donovan knew, but he just pretended not to. He was getting rich and had control of his people. It didn't matter much where the money came from.

Eric got to his feet and paced back and forth in front of the fire. "I can't believe I was so gullible. I believed Donovan's lies about the vigilantes. I even let him convince me my mom and dad and brother were against me." He closed his eyes and shook his head. "I should have known better. I grew up out there. Some of the guys might have been rednecks, but they'd never have turned on a neighbor."

"Donovan was a very convincing man," J.B. reassured him. "And a dangerous one." He sighed and leaned over to kiss Gram. "I'm just glad it's over and we all got out of there in one piece."

Gram smiled up at him. "If it wasn't for Jennie and Eric, we may not have survived at all."

Jennie got to her feet and went to stand beside Eric.

Slipping her arm around his waist, she added, "It was all supposed to happen like it did. And it happened for a reason. The plane crashed and—"

"Are you saying God made it crash?" Eric asked.

"No. I don't think God makes bad things happen. But He used the crash for good. We survived. I went for help and met you. None of us knew what was going on. Only God had the big picture."

"Well said, Jennie." Gram beamed at her.

"You have a cool granddaughter, Mrs. Bradley." Eric's gaze caught Jennie's and held. Suddenly she wasn't the least bit worried about Marilee.

"Hey, want to help me make dinner?" she asked.

"Sure." He settled an arm around her shoulder and gave her a teasing grin. "Got any tofu?"

Young Adult Fiction Series From Bethany House Publishers

(Ages 12 and up)

CHRISTY AND TODD: THE COLLEGE YEARS
by Robin Jones Gunn
Long-time fans of Christy Miller can now share in Christy's joys and struggles as her relationship with Todd blossoms.

GOLDEN FILLY SERIES
by Lauraine Snelling
Tricia Evanston races to become the first female jockey to win the sought-after Triple Crown.

JENNIE MCGRADY MYSTERIES
by Patricia Rushford
A contemporary Nancy Drew, Jennie McGrady's sleuthing talents bring back readers again and again.

LIVE! FROM BRENTWOOD HIGH
by Judy Baer
The staff of an action-packed teen-run news show explores the love, laughter, and tears of high school life.

PASSPORT TO DANGER
by Mary Reeves Bell
Constantine Rea, an American living in modern-day Austria, confronts the lasting horrors of the Holocaust.

UNMISTAKABLY COOPER ELLIS
by Wendy Lee Nentwig
Laugh and cry with Cooper as she strives to balance modeling, faith, and life at her Manhattan high school.